Murder at the Christmas Carols

The Wootton Windmill Mysteries
Book 1

Izzie Harper

ISBN 978-1-7392189-0-4

For Enid Blyton and Agatha Christie. Where it all started.

Chapter 1

DAY 1 – 21st Dec, 4pm

It was the week before Christmas and festivities were in full swing in the historic Kent village of Lower Wootton. On the village green, half a mile in from the coast, locals had gathered for the much-loved carols by candlelight. Children, parents and grandparents stood in huddles, coats fastened against the biting air, bobble hats pulled down. For once, the weather gods had obliged. Snow lay sleeping on tree branches and rooftops, and boots crunched on the white carpet underfoot. The vicar's wife was ladling out mulled wine and the baker had made a fresh batch of mince pies. Fruit and spice aromas wafted gloriously on the December air.

Outside the Windmill Inn, this year's giant fir tree stood proudly, a mass of twinkling fairy lights. It was an annual gift from a local garden centre. Next to it, a huge snowman glowed in the moonlight.

The church choir were standing by the white picket fence, dressed in their flowing cassocks and white surplices, belting out their last carol. Ellie Blix was in the middle of the group, felt reindeer horns tucked into the side of her wayward ponytail. She'd stopped singing for a breather and was listening. Her back and shoulders ached. Ten years ago, cleaning every day was a breeze, but today she had cleaned an office, done an Airbnb changeover and ironed more sheets than she'd ever thought possible. It didn't help that her daughter, Zoe, was still ill, and this meant Ellie's cleaning company was a staff member down.

'Hail the heaven-born Prince of Peace,' the choir sang. *'Hail the Sun of Righteousness.'* The descant soared, and with it, Ellie's spirits.

A huge moon glowed in the midnight-blue sky above.

'Light and life to all he brings, risen with healing in his wings.'

The choir conductor swung her forearm in time with the music.

'Mild he lays his glory by, born that man no more may die.'

Ellie looked up at the third floor of the windmill where she and Zoe lived. The striking landmark had been in her family for several generations, back to the days when it was used for milling wheat. The black weatherboarded tower stood on a brick base, and four white 'sails' were at the top.

In a tiny window, dark-haired Zoe was in her dressing gown, watching the carols below. She caught her mum's eye and waved excitedly. Ellie felt a flutter of pride, then tinges of anger. Damn glandular fever. One minute it had gone … then it was back with a vengeance. She grinned and waved back. Hopefully, next year would be easier for her and twenty-two-year-old Zoe.

Ellie glanced around her, basking in the familiar scene. She felt a warm glow of appreciation for the village where she was born, for the people she'd known all her life, the friends who had helped her through the last twelve months. The Rectory, where common sense and plain speaking were always in plentiful supply. The village shop, where wine was always in the fridge. The family butcher – who regularly left a brace of pheasants or rabbits at Ellie's front door to make sure she and Zoe were eating.

'Born to raise us from the earth, born to give them second birth.'

Suddenly, Ellie caught a glimpse of a young man and gasped. Unshaven. Tatty coat. Black beanie.

Finn.

What on earth was he doing back? Even at a distance, he had the same troubled energy as all those times when Dave had brought him home for a pep talk when he got into trouble.

'Hark! the Herald angels sing, Glory to the newborn King.'

The carol reached its final lines and fireworks erupted into the sky. For a few moments, the village green was a cacophony of loud bangs and dog barks, a kaleidoscope of flashing lights and smoke.

Ellie scoured the green for Finn, but he had disappeared into the crowd. Surely, she hadn't imagined seeing him?

There was a frenzy of clapping. Gradually, the lights and noise receded, and quiet enveloped the village green. Suddenly, behind Ellie, there was a loud groan and then a thud as something hit the ground.

Ellie spun round.

A woman was on her back, surplice and cassock splayed around her, song sheets scattered on the snow.

'Andrea?' Ellie leaned over her. She wasn't moving. Maybe she'd fainted?

There was a scurry of locals.

'Is there a first-aider here?' someone shouted. 'Can we get some help?'

'Andrea?' Ellie didn't know what to do.

The woman still didn't rouse.

'Dr Peters is coming,' a voice said.

Ellie kneeled and examined Andrea's face. It was pale and still. Until last week, the two of them hadn't been this close up for twenty-five years. An image flashed through her mind of Andrea yelling through the windmill's letterbox, banging at the door, demanding to speak to her.

The owner of the village shop was beside Ellie now. 'She went down like a lead balloon, didn't she?' She was gabbling. 'When we had tea earlier, Andrea said her stomach was hurting. Perhaps something disagreed with her.'

Ellie clambered to her feet.

Another woman arrived, red in the face and puffing. Tall and elegantly dressed in a green cloak with a hood, it was Martha, Andrea's best friend. 'Get away from her,' she snarled at Ellie. 'Don't you think you did enough last week?'

Ellie shrank back, embarrassment coursing through her.

Martha kneeled beside her friend's body. 'Andrea? What's happened?'

Dr Peters arrived, still in his cassock and surplice. 'Martha, if I may?' He crouched on the ground. 'Andrea? Can you hear me?' He placed his hand on her chest, then leaned over and put his ear to her mouth. Then he placed his fingers on her neck.

Ellie knew these weren't good signs.

Dr Peters began resuscitation.

Martha let out a wail.

'Shall I call 999?' Ellie reached under her clothing layers and retrieved her phone.

The doctor felt Andrea's pulse again and listened for breathing. 'Yes, please.' He continued with a few more rounds of resuscitation, then stopped. He looked up at the crowd that had gathered and very gently shook his head.

Chapter 2

6pm

Gladys Blackman's frail frame was a stick in the doorway of her 1970s bungalow, her Crimplene trousers and top a flimsy barrier against the cold air. She was in her seventies and lived on her own in a quiet cul-de-sac ten minutes away from the high street.

Ellie heaved her vacuum cleaner into the boot of her jeep for the sixth time that day.

'Have a great Christm–' Gladys' face fell, presumably realising the tactlessness of what she was about to say. 'Oh, sorry.' She clenched her jaw in solidarity and waved crossed fingers at Ellie. 'Hope this one is a bit better for you and young Zoe.' She smiled. 'It was kind of you to drop off the food. *And* to help me with the hoovering.'

'You're very welcome. Can't stuff my face knowing you've got nothing. Especially if your grandchildren are coming.' Ellie yanked the reindeer horns off her head and lobbed them on top of all her cleaning gear. 'I'll ping Social Services an email about your cleaner too when I have a minute.' She slammed the door shut and let out a huge sigh.

Gladys waved cheerily. 'Bye, dear.'

Ellie clambered into the old jeep. On the seat next to her was an assortment of goodies, all gifts from customers: juniper gin from the off-licence; reindeer donuts from Kathy at the bakery; and a box of mince pies which she'd already opened.

She was soon driving home. The narrow lanes snaked round what was once an agricultural village, built in the twelfth century around a manor house, church and farm. Snow was still falling, and the jeep's wheels made fresh tracks.

Thoughts of Andrea kept drifting into Ellie's mind. They might not have been close since their row in sixth form, but it was still hard to take in that she was dead. They'd continued to live in the same village, uttering a grunt or a mutter if they collided in the supermarket aisles, but Andrea had stuck to her vow never to speak to Ellie again. And then, last week Andrea had turned up at the windmill, totally out of the blue. Their strange exchange had stuck in Ellie's mind. It came back to her now as clearly as if it had been yesterday.

She had arrived home from work, exhausted, knees sore from scrubbing a tiled floor, praying the heating engineer had fixed the boiler.

And there was Andrea, waiting for her when she got out of the jeep.

No 'Hello', or 'How are you?' Just, 'Did you get the email I sent last week?'

It felt like an ambush, the question an accusation. Especially as they hadn't really spoken for so long.

Ellie hadn't seen an email. 'Perhaps it went into my spam folder,' she suggested. 'I'll have a look later. My daughter's not well. Her temperature shot up last night and the heating's on the blink.' She had tried to explain.

'But I need to talk to you,' Andrea insisted. 'It's not fair to blank me like this.'

Ellie tried to contain her irritation. Something must've happened. Trouble was, she didn't have the bandwidth to cope, to take on any more. 'I'm not blanking you. We haven't spoken for twenty-five years, for goodness' sake.'

Beside the village green, pub customers were bundling out of shiny Range Rovers and BMWs. They stared nosily, commenting and sniggering. Next door, her neighbour peered round the curtains.

It felt like everyone was watching.

But Andrea *still* wouldn't give up. She stomped up the path behind Ellie, out of breath and puffing. 'Oh, that's right. Just like you were at school.' She was raising her voice. 'Always thinking you were better than me.'

That hurt.

Ellie had never felt that way – and neither had Andrea. In fact, until Andrea ended their friendship, because Dave had dumped her for Ellie, the two of them had been close friends.

'Andrea, whatever this is about, I'm not going to discuss it here. Leave it with me. OK?' And she went inside.

But it didn't stop there.

CLACK. CLACK. CLACK. Andrea pushed open the letter box and shouted, 'Let me in. I need to talk to you.'

What on earth was she thinking, turning up like this?

Ellie was about to reply when the letter box was thrust open again. 'You really are a selfish cow, aren't you?' Andrea screamed.

So much for sitting down and putting her feet up.

Ellie strode towards the door and opened it. Said to Andrea, 'This is embarrassing for everyone. I'm not inviting you in so could you please stop shouting through my letterbox and go home.'

And, when she turned round, as if things couldn't possibly get any worse, Dave's mother, Sylvia, was a few feet away, staring at Ellie. She had a throw draped round her and was clutching a hot water bottle. 'Hope you don't mind,' she said sheepishly. 'I was hoping I could stay for a few days. My house is freezing.' She glanced over her shoulder. 'Do you think the engineer will have fixed the boiler soon?'

Ellie *did* mind. She would've liked to have been asked.

And now she felt guilty. If only Andrea had arrived at a better time. Because, whatever she had wanted, Ellie would never know.

In the snowy lane, a hatchback slowed to pass by. The driver waved at Ellie. It was the owner of the local garage.

Ellie's phone rang through the Bluetooth system.

'Hey, Mum,' Zoe said, her voice croaky from the glandular fever. 'You've been ages.'

'I'll be home in about ten minutes. Grab a quick bite then I'm due at the pub. How are you feeling?'

'Awful. I can hardly swallow. And my temperature's back.'

'You did the right thing then, staying indoors for the carols. Keep warm and drink plenty of water.'

'If I drink any more, my bladder will burst.' She forced a brave laugh. 'I've been phoning you. I saw Andrea collapse on the green. How is she? Dr Peters and the ambulance were there.' Zoe's words tumbled out.

'She's dead, love, I'm sorry to say.'

Zoe gasped. 'What happened?'

'I don't know. The doctors will run tests.' Finn's image flashed through Ellie's mind. 'And bizarrely, Finn's back. He was at the carols.'

'Who?'

'Andrea's son.' Zoe must be tired. 'Don't you remember him from school?'

'Oh. Him.'

'Looked dreadful.' Ellie changed gears to go round a corner. 'Anyway, I won't be long. We can talk when I get home. Try not to think about Andrea. Is Gran with you?'

'No, she went to meet a friend. They were going to watch the carols. When are the Airbnb guests arriving?'

'They cancelled earlier so it'll be just us three for Christmas.' She didn't say she was gutted to lose the money; how much splitting with Zoe's dad had affected her financially; how worried she was about not being able to keep the windmill without Dave's salary.

'Oh, Mum. Sorry.' Zoe must have caught the frustration in her mother's voice. 'Do you want me to ask Dad to help out?'

'Thanks, lovey. He's offered, but we'll manage without his money.' Ellie changed tack. 'Have you been resting?'

'Not really. I wanted to make things nice for when you get home. I know you said you didn't want any decorations this year but...' She put on a silly voice, 'They look so priddy.'

'Oh, love.'

'And Gran and I have made cinnamon buns. Some celebrity chef was making them on the telly earlier.' Zoe paused. Took a gulp. 'By the way – you mentioned Christmas Day so, before I forget ... and in case you hear it from Simon. Or someone else...'

Ellie braced herself, wondering what was coming. She rammed the jeep into third gear as she accelerated up the hill towards the village.

'...Dad has moved into his new place.'

Ellie's stomach did a somersault. She tugged at the scarf round her neck, suddenly flushing hot all over. She should be past this by now. It had been a year since the breakup.

'Mum?' Zoe's words became faint and fragmented. 'Mum, are you still there?'

'Sorry. Lost you for a moment. He's what?'

'...moved into his new flat. And he's asked if I want to come for Christmas. Simon's going to be there with his girlfriend. They've got a puppy.'

Ellie muttered under her breath. She slowed the car and pulled onto the verge. Pushed the gearbox into neutral and reduced the volume on the radio. She tried to steady her voice, just as she'd done every time she'd talked to Zoe about her father in the last year. 'I didn't...' She searched for something neutral to say while she absorbed the news. 'I didn't know your brother had got a puppy.'

Ellie opened the window, letting her eyelids close briefly. Remember. Don't make Zoe choose.

She let the cold air soothe her inner turmoil, keeping her voice low. 'You must do what you want, love.'

'No, Mum. I'm not leaving you with Gran. I've told Dad no.'

There were a few moments' silence.

'Simon and Jen are going, so Dad'll have company. This is the first year since–'

'Yes, well, let's not go into that again.' The thought filled her with dread. 'See how you feel. You might want to pop round there for a few hours. I can understand you wanting to see your dad and brother. Swap presents? And who could resist a puppy?' Ellie closed the car window. She wanted the conversation to be over. Dave was her childhood sweetheart, and his betrayal had been the hardest thing in her life. 'I'll be home shortly. We can talk later.' She shifted the gears into first. 'Stay in the warm.'

And as she continued her drive, she found it hard not to wonder where Dave had moved to – and whether he was living alone.

Chapter 3

7.30pm

The news of Andrea's death had ripped through the village and the Windmill Inn was busier than Ellie had ever seen it. In one of the bay windows, a large tree stood floor to ceiling, a mass of fairy lights, tinsel and baubles. Both fireplaces had open fires and were belching out heat. Staff scuttled about with plates from the kitchen. Steaming lasagnes. Steak and ale pie with puff pastry. Lobster and chips.

Under the low beams of the sixteenth-century building, carols tinkled over the music system. Everything might have looked normal, but it wasn't. Voices reverberated everywhere, and there was one topic of conversation: Andrea.

Ellie was serving drinks behind the bar, covering Zoe's shift while she was recovering. Her best friend, Sally – who was the village dressmaker – was standing at the bar with her rescue dog, Luna, and her *alleged* platonic friend, Pete – the garden centre owner and annual donor of the village Christmas tree. Like many of the villagers, Pete's family originated in Wootton. His ancestors had worked at the manor house and on the farm.

'Zoe still not better?' Sally asked. She adjusted the strap on her dungarees and folded up her coat.

Ellie shook her head. It wasn't Zoe's fault she wasn't well, but on top of Ellie's cleaning business, and the Airbnb guests at the windmill, she was struggling to manage her daughter's bar shifts.

'The usual?' she asked Sally.

Sally gave a thumbs-up.

Ellie noticed the mistletoe that was hanging from one of the beams over the bar. She poured prosecco into a flute and a pint for Pete. 'Aww. Look. You two are under the mistletoe. How apt.' She placed their drinks on the bar.

Sally and Pete jumped apart, like they'd burnt each other, giggling furtively.

'I see you've still got Sylvia staying.' Sally grinned mischievously and gestured to Ellie's mother-in-law, who'd arrived last week 'for a couple of days'. Cheeks glowing, Sylvia was busy chatting to the women from the Bakery Book Club who were having their Christmas party.

On the table in front of her was a half-drunk glass of white wine and a full one.

'She can't afford to heat her place while it's really cold, so I didn't really feel like I could say no. She told Zoe she 'rather likes it here' so I'm not sure how I'm going to despatch her back home.' Ellie rolled her eyes.

'I'm sure she does.' Sally chuckled and threw a sideways glance at Pete. 'Why isn't she staying with her son and heir?'

'They don't get on. Something about the police. I'm very fond of her, and Zoe loves having her gran around, but I swear if she reorganises one more of my cupboards, she'll be out on her ear. And she has the central heating on at 23 degrees all day. My bills were through the roof *before* she arrived.'

'Oh, the irony. I'd ship her off to Dave's whether they get on or not.' Sally changed the subject. 'Thank goodness Dr Peters was at the carols. Did Andrea have a heart attack or something?' She sipped her prosecco.

Behind them, locals were deep in conversation.

'Don't know. Presumably there will be a postmortem.'

'What an awful thing to happen. Her poor family. Just before Christmas too.'

Ellie was gathering empty glasses and stacking them in the dishwasher. 'You know, I can't get her face out of my mind. She looked grey.' Regret seeped into her tone. 'It feels weird. Having not spoken to her properly since sixth form, I've no idea what's been going on for her.'

'It's not just you, Ells. She hasn't really spoken to me since then either.' Sally's voice was thick with emotion. 'When something like this happens, you realise how petty so many arguments are.'

Ellie avoided Sally's eyes.

Pete lowered his voice. He was a gentle man who radiated kindness and good humour. 'Perhaps she had a stroke? She definitely hasn't been herself lately. She's had a few rows with locals. Bit my head off when she came to get plants from the garden centre and she's been furious with how we've done her gardening for a number of months now, even though we did exactly what she asked for.' He swigged his pint, evidently savouring the brew from local Hawkshill Brewery.

'Oh dear.' Ellie's face was sympathetic. 'That might explain her turning up at my place last week then.' She shook her head and groaned with embarrassment. 'Half the families in the village must've seen us.'

'I'm sure they loved it,' Sally teased affectionately.

Ellie grunted.

'What did her email say?'

'Not much. Just that she had something to tell me and asked if we could meet up. I meant to reply, but what with everything that was going on, I completely forgot.' She opened the bar hatch and walked round to the customer side, dabbing unenthusiastically at the bar with a cloth. She had been on her feet since 7am, and her legs and back were still aching. 'If you contact someone out of the blue – after twenty-five years – and say you've got something important to tell them, you've got to expect you might not get a great reaction. Especially if you've had a falling out.' Ellie glanced from Sally to Pete. 'If they don't answer, it doesn't give you the right to pitch up at their home and demand to come in.'

'Who knows what goes through people's brains.' Sally placed her glass down with a clunk.

'Now, of course, I can see she was desperate to talk to me about something. I feel really guilty.' Ellie straightened chairs and shuffled over to the fireplace.

'I said at the time you should have heard her out,' Sally said. 'But – it's done now. Don't feel bad.'

Kathy, the local baker, was moving towards the door with her husband.

Sally handed Pete Luna's lead and followed Ellie, watching as her friend added logs to the dwindling fire. Sally stacked a few pint glasses and tucked them under her arm. In a gentle voice, she said, 'You know, I've never understood why the pair of you didn't put that stupid row behind you. We were all hormonal teenagers, for goodness' sake. *Everyone* fell out in sixth form.'

'I know, but, for some reason, not as spectacularly as Andrea and me.' Ellie brushed wood dust from her hands. This wasn't a topic she liked thinking about. 'And *she* started the whole row. I was busy being excited about having just got engaged.' She shook her head in irritation. 'What I cannot understand is, after all this time, why contact me now?'

Sally shrugged. 'Something must've happened. But you weren't to know she was going to collapse at the carols.' She stroked Luna's ears.

Ellie exhaled loudly and mopped spills off the bar with a cloth. 'Martha is never going to forgive me. Anyone would think I'd killed Andrea myself, the way she was with me earlier.' She told Sally and Pete what Martha had said.

'They've been best friends for years. Martha moved here when her son died. I get the impression she's quite protective of Andrea.' Sally sipped her drink and nicked one of Pete's crisps.

'I can vouch for that,' Pete added. 'She brought Andrea up to the garden centre last week to choose her Christmas tree, and Martha insisted on carrying everything for her.

She was fussing over Andrea like she was her mum, or something.'

'Well, friends are meant to care about each other...' Sally pulled a silly face at Ellie, and they both giggled.

Pete gestured to the table where Kathy and her husband had been sitting. 'C'mon, Sal. Let's grab those seats. Let Ellie get on with her job. Poor Luna keeps getting her tail trodden on.'

Sally handed Ellie the empties and placed her hand on her friend's shoulder. 'Someone's left their book behind.' She picked the paperback up and passed it to Ellie. 'Catch you later, hun,' she shouted in Ellie's direction and went off with Pete.

Ellie noticed the cover. *The Canterbury Murders.* Kathy's book group was reading it. It was probably one of theirs. She opened the cover to see if it had a name in it. In black ink, the owner had written their name.

Martha McVey.

Chapter 4

10pm

A couple of hours later, Ellie was crunching through the snow on the village green towards the windmill. Where the choir had sung, a police forensics tent now stood. Instead of the pretty fairy lights of a few hours ago, blue and white crime scene tape billowed in the wind. The police must've thought the death was suspicious.

Ellie lengthened her stride towards home. She couldn't shift the image from her mind of Andrea, lying on the snow. And Finn, her son. Why had he turned up at the carols out of the blue and disappeared like that? Did he know his mum had died? Someone had to check he was OK. If Zoe was ever in the same situation, she hoped someone would look after her. She would nip round to Andrea's and see if he was there.

The windmill was in darkness when she arrived. She opened the front door, listened for signs that Zoe was still up.

Nothing. She must have gone to bed.

Ellie tiptoed in and headed for the office, not bothering to take her coat and shoes off.

Rebus jumped out of his bed and bounded over to Ellie, who shut the door and fussed over him briefly, keen not to wake Zoe.

She strode over to the cleaning company safe. This was where she kept the keys for all her customers' houses. Opening it, she unhooked a set of keys labelled 'Andrea Burdett' and dropped them into her coat pocket. Ellie grabbed Rebus' lead from the rack by the door and the two of them headed straight out again.

When Andrea had contracted Blix Blitz Cleaning Services, it was on the understanding that Ellie would *never* do her cleaning. So, five minutes later when she and Rebus arrived at Andrea's home, it was the first time she had seen the rambling seventeenth-century stone building up close. It was even more stunning than Ellie's staff had described. Two roads back from the high street, the Priest House was tastefully lit at the front by tall, black streetlamps, and had been part of the old Catholic convent and chapel.

Ellie opened the creaky wrought iron gate and walked up the path. Rebus scuffled about in the undergrowth, sniffing out interesting smells and following movement. Meowing sounds caught Ellie's attention. A tabby cat sauntered out of the bushes, carefree and aloof.

'Hey, little one. My staff have told me about you. You're Mouse, aren't you?' Ellie crouched down and petted the cat, which purred loudly. 'Let's go inside, shall we? Find Finn?'

Ellie called Rebus and got to her feet. She followed the path around the side of the house and was reaching for the handle on the gate, when she heard a door bang.

Ellie froze.

'Finn? Is that you? It's Ellie. Ellie Blix.' She inched forward.

A motorbike engine started up. Revved loudly. Tyres screeched, and the bike accelerated away.

Was it Finn? Ellie was puzzled. She put her hand out for the dog and clicked her fingers. 'Rebus. Here, boy. C'mon. Let's double-check he's not here, shall we?' She reached into her pocket and produced Andrea's house keys. When she got to the door, she knocked and called out.

Inside the house, the lights had been left on, curtains closed.

'Hello? Finn? Anyone?'

There was no reply.

The room was open plan. Up one end, there was a large oak table, cream kitchen cabinets and a butler-style sink.

Ellie surveyed the scene. There was no sign of Mouse. Rebus scuffled about on the floor. She picked up an open envelope addressed to Andrea and popped it on the kitchen table. A Christmas card, presumably.

Pans hung from elegant wrought iron hooks on the ceiling. Crockery lay in rows on wooden shelves. On the worktop by the sink, four side plates were stacked with chocolate cake crumbs on them. Next to these was a patisserie box from Wootton Bakery, Kathy's place.

On the other side of the room, an old desktop monitor glowed in the dark.

Ellie went straight over. She spotted a black beanie on the bureau next to the computer. It was the one Finn always wore. Beside this lay a half-empty packet of chewing gum and a small pile of business cards. Staring up at her were the words, FINN BURDETT – GARDENER, with his mobile number.

On the computer monitor, Andrea's Gmail account was open, displaying an email. The person who'd just left must have been reading it. Ellie's gaze fell on the message which was addressed to her:

Please, Ellie.

I'm sorry about coming round. I can see it was a mistake. I know you don't want to talk to me, but I need to tell you something important.

It's not just about you and me.

Other people are involved.

Can we please meet before it's too late?

Andrea x

'Oh, my goodness,' Ellie said out loud in the room, recoiling from the monitor. She must've written this after she came round to the windmill.

Ellie reread the text. What on earth could she have wanted to tell me? What did she mean, *before it's too late?*

And what other people?

Her imagination was darting all over the place. What was bothering her most of all was whether these things were separate and a coincidence – or whether they were connected with Andrea's death.

Chapter 5

10.30pm

Back home again, Ellie was sitting cross-legged on the sofa, trying to force down some tomato soup which she didn't really want. Sylvia was still at the pub, and Zoe was in bed, so she had the place to herself. As she cradled the bowl in her hands, she was mulling over the day's events.

Andrea's death.

The unsent email.

Dave's new flat.

Sadness pulled at her like an invisible cord. Andrea's death had shaken her dreadfully. They'd known each other all their life. Same playgroup. Same junior and secondary school. And before she and Sally became friends, Ellie and Andrea had been inseparable. Somehow, it made things worse that they'd been estranged for so long. There were literally huge chunks of Andrea's life that Ellie knew nothing about, unless relayed to her by other people.

Sadly, that was what happened when people fell out. And, when Ellie and Dave had got engaged in sixth form, Andrea had accused Ellie of 'stealing' him and had vowed never to speak to her again. It was a vow she'd stuck to.

Ellie gave up on the soup and placed the bowl on the coffee table, then padded up the wooden spiral staircase to the first floor, trying to make as little noise as possible so as not to wake Zoe. She entered the bathroom and ran the water, glugging bubble bath into the steaming tub.

Crossing the landing to Zoe's bedroom, she peered around the door, expecting to see her daughter tucked up in bed. But the duvet was flat, not a crease in sight. Pink and purple scatter cushions lay neatly against the head rest.

'The little minx,' Ellie muttered, then shouted up the spiral staircase: 'Zoe? Are you in my room?'

Sometimes Zoe got into Ellie's bed when she was feeling wobbly.

Rebus bounded in and leapt onto Zoe's empty bed, then dashed up to the second floor.

Ellie followed him upstairs into her own bedroom.

Nothing.

Sylvia had temporarily taken up residence in Simon's room, but there wasn't a peep of anyone in there either.

She had pushed Simon's portable speakers and baseball cap to one side and laid out her hairbrush and comb, perfume, moisturiser and vitamins, all in a neat row.

Ellie went back down the stairs into Zoe's bedroom. Her daughter took her phone everywhere and there was no sign of it. It was worrying to think she had glandular fever and she'd gone out in the freezing snow.

Ellie perched on the bed while Rebus stared at her, whining.

'Where would someone with a temperature go?' Ellie got her phone out and dialled Zoe. 'Pick up. Pick up.'

It went to voicemail.

'Hi, love. Just Mum, to see where you are. I've ... er ... got home and you aren't here. Give me a quick buzz, would you, or a text? Let me know you're alright? Thanks. Love you.'

Ellie's attention was drawn to a photograph on her daughter's dressing table. In it, Zoe hung round her dad's shoulders from behind, her slender arms round his neck, their cheeks close, both relaxed and happy. Dave's eyes shone with love.

Ellie sniffed and wiped her nose. She stared at her phone and dabbed at her eyes. Was this it? Everyone said she and Dave would get back together. But that hadn't happened. Worst of all, they weren't even friends any more. Best friends since school – and now they couldn't even talk to each other.

If she rang him, would he answer? What if he *had* met someone? Maybe he'd moved into his new flat with a new partner? Ellie shook her head determinedly and said out loud, 'You're tired. You are *not* going to phone him. You're not.'

Hearing Ellie's sniffles, Rebus jumped onto Ellie's lap and she enveloped the dog in a hug.

But the photo of Zoe and Dave had got her thinking about Finn and Andrea. What had happened for the two of them to become estranged? Where was Finn's father? Did he know about Andrea's death? A worrying thought hit her. Was it possible that Andrea's death had something to do with him?

Suddenly, Rebus shot off Ellie's lap and amidst a frenzy of barking, he scurried downstairs. A whoosh of cold air came up.

'Only me,' Sylvia shouted up. 'I've had quite the evening.' Her words were slurred. 'And heard something *very* interesting about Andrea.' She hiccupped loudly.

Oh, joy. Sylvia was tiddly.

Quick. Get in the bath.

'Yoo-hoo. Ellie? Zoe? Where are you?'

Chapter 6

11pm

By the time Sylvia got back to the windmill, she was ravenous. After a glass of wine too many in the pub, a bit of grease would go down a treat. She moved the toaster and plugged it in by the kettle. It made much more sense to have it there. When the bread was golden, she spread a thick layer of butter on it and piled liver pâté on top. She didn't drink alcohol usually. Only on special occasions, but after the shocking news of Andrea's death, everyone had been knocking back the booze in the pub, and Sylvia had allowed herself to be influenced. Not that it took much. If she was honest, she was enjoying the company that Ellie's house and village gave her. It was lonely living alone, and she still missed her late husband.

Sylvia sat at the kitchen table to eat her snack. Her thoughts quickly drifted to Ellie. She was upstairs in the bath, hopefully having a good soak. Over the last week, Sylvia had seen first-hand how exhausted Ellie was, trying to juggle jobs and look after Zoe. Thank goodness Zoe had got in touch and asked her to come and give them a hand. Given it was Sylvia's son who had broken up the family, she knew she was the last person Ellie would ask for help. But Ellie was having financial problems and Sylvia wanted to help. It hadn't been a lie to say she was struggling to pay her heating bills during this cold snap of weather. The blasted things had sky-rocketed for everyone in recent months. It just wasn't the full story. She couldn't bear the thought that her daughter-in-law might lose the windmill. It was a truly stunning building, but it didn't seem to have a speck of insulation and had more draughts than a corridor.

Sylvia was finishing her pâté when the front door opened. Barks erupted from upstairs, and Rebus scrambled down to greet Zoe.

'Hey, Gran,' Zoe said as she came in. 'That smells good.' She shouted up the stairwell, 'Mum? I'm back. Be up in a sec.' She took her coat off and clomped up the stairs. If only Ellie would carpet the darn things. The place would be much quieter.

Sylvia followed Zoe up, eager to share what she had heard in the pub. Zoe was standing in the doorway to the bathroom, glowing from the cold air, clutching three packets of crisps. She was wearing baggy joggers tucked into cream Ugg boots, and a hoodie.

'Didn't you get my voicemail?' Ellie asked Zoe.

Sylvia caught the concern in Ellie's voice.

'No. When?' Zoe produced her phone from her pocket and swiped the screen to check her messages. 'Oh, gosh. Missed it. Sorry, Mum.'

'What about the awful throat and temperature you were telling me about earlier? It's midnight. Where have you been?' Ellie wedged her pen and notepad between the taps.

Sylvia was a mother herself. She understood Ellie's worry.

'I fancied some crisps and went to the garage. Not a crime, is it? I put my coat and scarf on.' Zoe swung the bags in the air. 'Cheese and onion. Got you and Gran some too, but if you're going to moan at me, I'll eat yours myself.' She changed the subject. 'Any news on what happened to Andrea?'

'No.'

'I can't believe it, can you?' Zoe thumped down on the toilet seat.

'It's all everyone was talking about in the pub.' Sylvia could feel herself swaying slightly and put her hand out to steady herself. 'I've got to tell you what–'

‘Check you out, Gran.’ Zoe threw her head back and cackled with laughter. ‘Have you been on the sherry?’

‘That wine must’ve been stronger than it looked.’

‘Park yourself there, look.’ Zoe got up and steered her gran towards the loo seat. Sitting cross-legged on the tiles, she faced her mum and slapped her forehead in a ‘silly me’ gesture. ‘Of course. The pub. You were doing my shift. I’m sorry, Mum. I’m going to ask Maggie and Tom if they can get someone else to cover me. It’s too much for you with the cleaning business too, especially since you’re a staff member down with me being ill.’

‘Thank you. That’d be a great help. And if you’re still not better after Christmas, I’m going to hire a cover cleaner.’

This was the first time Sylvia had heard Ellie admit she needed help. ‘Perhaps I can do some of the admin.’ Sylvia hiccupped.

‘You need some water, Gran.’

Ellie snorted at her daughter’s honesty.

Sylvia pretended not to have heard Zoe’s remark. ‘I'm happy to help with the bookkeeping too maybe?’

‘That would be great. Thank you. I can’t go on like this.’ She spoke to Zoe now. ‘I’m exhausted. I think it’s why I was freaked out when I got home and you weren’t here.’

'Aww. Did you think I'd been kidnapped? Or abducted by aliens?'

Ellie and Zoe giggled.

'Something like that.'

Sylvia hoped this was a phase that Ellie would get through. She had a great relationship with both her children, and she was a grafter. From what she could tell, the cleaning business was thriving. The problem was that Ellie didn't have enough staff and was doing too much herself.

'Must admit, though,' Ellie added. 'I'd been over to Andrea's and got a bit freaked out there too.'

'Wait. You've been to Andrea's house?' Zoe's voice was shrill. 'Why?'

Sylvia tutted loudly and covered her ears. 'You don't have to shriek.'

Ellie didn't answer. Her expression was sheepish.

'There's crime scene tape and a CSI tent.' Zoe ignored her gran's plea. 'The police must think Andrea was killed.'

'Oh dear.' Sylvia knew how the police worked. Like Dave, her husband had been in CID. 'After your row last week, and your feud, you would have been a person of interest anyway. But I'm sorry to say, your little visit will have made that worse.'

*

Fifteen minutes later, Sylvia was on the sofa, knitting away happily. After a pint of water, her hiccups had gone. Ellie was next to her, in her bathrobe, towelling her hair dry. Zoe was in her pyjamas, curled up in an armchair, stuffing crisps.

'OK, OK. It was a bit impetuous, I suppose,' Ellie said begrudgingly.

'Stupid, more like,' Zoe muttered under her breath.

Ellie chucked the towel onto the coffee table. 'I wanted to see if I could help. Finn was at the carols briefly and left before the end. I wasn't sure if he knew his mum was dead. And I feel really guilty for not contacting Andrea once I'd read her email.'

Sylvia noted Zoe staring at Ellie, a strange look on her face.

'Until this afternoon, I didn't know Finn was back,' Ellie continued. 'I'm guessing he must be staying there.'

Sylvia listened while Ellie told them about the person leaving as she arrived, about Finn's belongings and the draft email.

'I can only assume he was reading it just before he left. It's a pretty ancient computer. There was no lock screen.'

Zoe tutted loudly. 'What if it had been a serial killer waiting to bump you off?'

'Now whose imagination is in overdrive?' Sylvia asked. 'You've been watching too much TV.'

'Well, speaking of TV… Seriously, Mum. We've watched enough *Midsomer Murders*. The first thing the police ask is if the victim had any enemies.'

'We weren't *enemies*. We just didn't talk.'

'Zoe's right,' said Sylvia. 'The detectives will ask about recent disputes and long-term feuds.'

'See? Tell her, Gran. You'll definitely be a suspect. Dad's going to do his nut.'

Ellie screwed up her face in embarrassment.

'You know what? I try really hard not to take sides with you and Dad, but in this case, if he's annoyed with you, I don't blame him.' Zoe stared at her mum. 'Were you looking for Finn, or did you go over there deliberately to annoy Dad?'

Ellie opened her mouth, presumably to protest, and closed it. She stretched her arm out and pulled her daughter towards her. 'Sorry if you've felt caught in the crossfire. I've tried hard to stop that from happening.'

'I know. Generally, I haven't. Just occasionally.'

'It wasn't the smartest move, but I can see why you did it,' Sylvia said to Ellie. 'And it's done now. The trouble is, it could look like you have something to hide. Or that you went to Andrea's to remove something before the police got there.'

Ellie groaned.

'I would suggest the three of us sit down and come up with a plan, and find out what happened to Andrea as quickly as we can – before my son and his colleagues are at the door.' Sylvia gave Zoe a stern look.

'Us? Investigate?' Zoe didn't sound at all enthusiastic.

'Not formally. But your mother needs our help, and a bit of Miss Marple-ing wouldn't hurt.'

'I suppose,' Zoe said reluctantly.

'We can be Blix Investigators.' Sylvia gave them an infectious grin.

'Oh, my goodness. *Blix Investigators*.' Excitement gleamed in Zoe's eyes. 'I *love* that name. It's so cool. In that case, I'm in.'

'No wonder you and Dave clash, Sylvia.' Ellie laughed. 'Like mother, like son.'

'How very dare you,' Sylvia said jokingly. 'Although, actually ... it *was* me who got him into mysteries. We used to watch them together after school and try to work out the clues. I always preferred Miss Marple, and he was a Sherlock Holmes fan.'

'I didn't know you and Dad don't get on.' Zoe had her mother's sharp mind. Never missed a thing. 'Why not?'

'It's a long story. The short version is that – for reasons I won't go into now – I didn't want him to go into the police–'

'I never knew that,' said Ellie. 'I knew it was something to do with the police, but that's all he's ever said.'

'His view has always been that I'm unsupportive of him.' It was much more complex than that, but Sylvia didn't want to discuss it further now. 'Back to Andrea's death.' Her mind was already running ahead. 'I've got my social work experience.' She considered Ellie for a moment. 'Your mother has everyone confiding in her.' She turned to Zoe. 'So, Madam. What's your superpower?'

'Ooh. Dunno. Research? Tech stuff? The internet?'

'That's a relief. I hate technology. Right. I need my bed.' Sylvia was about to get up. 'I nearly forgot. I learnt something interesting about Andrea earlier. Linda, the butcher's wife, told me. Andrea was ill. Did you know?'

'What? No.'

'She'd been diagnosed with a malignant brain tumour. Inoperable, I believe.'

Chapter 7

DAY 2 - 22nd Dec, 8am

The next morning, Ellie was out of the house by 7.45am, leaving Zoe asleep and Sylvia nursing a minor hangover. By 8am, she was at the counter in Matthews' Butchers in the high street. It was an old-fashioned butcher with huge chiller cabinets. Not a shred of clingfilm in sight, just trays of freshly cut meat from local farms. An honesty box nestled in a wicker basket of local farm eggs on the cabinet top. Through the shop window, the queue of customers trailed down the street. All eager to collect their turkey, sausages and ham. Ellie spotted the choir conductor, the vicar's wife and the pub landlord.

Nick Matthews, the owner, was bringing out the orders from the back. Charlie, his twenty-two-year-old son, was at the counter serving. In his white butcher's coat, his short, black, spiky hair was striking.

'Morning,' said Ellie. 'I've come to pick up Mrs Symonds' order, please?'

'Coming up,' Charlie replied. 'Dad? Mrs Symonds?' And to Ellie, 'How're you keeping, Mrs Blix?'

'Ellie, please. Hectic, as usual. I'm still taking in the news about Andrea.'

'Awful. She was only in here yesterday morning. She switched her order from a turkey crown to a big turkey, sausages and a ham joint.'

'Oh, no. That's so sad.' Did that mean she was expecting Finn to stay? Perhaps she had guests coming. 'Sorry if this seems nosey, but have you seen Finn the last couple of days? I know you guys were friends at school.'

'No.' A frown flickered on his face. 'I haven't.'

'He didn't tell you he was coming back for Christmas?'

Charlie shook his head. 'We lost touch a while ago. He was doing crazy things, angry about his family all the time. Why do you ask?'

'He came to the carols yesterday. Left before they finished.'

Nick, appeared from the back of the shop with several plastic bags. White coat, boots and a cloth cap on hair that was more speckled with grey than Charlie's. Stockier than his son too.

'Morning, Ellie. Dreadful news about Andrea. Just adding to what Charlie said, she told me she had her sister and brother-in-law, and Finn, coming for Christmas. That's why she changed her order. Excited about it, she was, too.'

'What a dreadful shame.'

'Quite a change because, the last I heard, she'd kicked Finn out. Really annoyed about it, Finn was. They hadn't got on for years, and she was fed up with him continually getting into trouble with the police.'

Nick handed bulging bags to Ellie. 'Here you go. That's for Mrs Symonds. Now, you won't forget to collect your own order, will you?'

'I haven't put one in.' Ellie was packing the bags of meat into her shopping bag.

'Good thing Sylvia did, then, isn't it? It's ready when you are.' Nick was beaming. 'Going back to Finn, poor lad...' He dropped his voice.

Ellie leaned a bit closer.

'Years ago, Andrea told my Linda that Finn's father had refused to have anything to do with him.'

Chapter 8

10.30am

Ellie was in the Hamilton's oast house, half a mile out of the village. It was a beautiful, two-storey, ragstone building with four conical vented roof kilns, one of a few traditional oasts in the area that had been used to dry hops for the local brewery.

In the hour and a half that she had been working her magic, she had transformed the oast house from stinking, morning-after-the-party mayhem to a tidy, fresh-smelling family home. It was the second time that the Hamilton's much-loved son, Drew, had thrown an impromptu party while his parents were away. Skiing this time. Ellie had finished in the nick of time and – unlike the last occasion when one of Drew's mates had thrown up on his parents' bed – with no disasters or telltale signs.

The reindeer horns were back on Ellie's head, but after the late night with Zoe and Sylvia, fatigue pulled at her whole body.

The clock on the mantlepiece said it was 10.29am.

She needed to get her skates on.

She quickly switched off the hoover, unplugged it and carried it to the hall. Opening the front door, she was leaning over, about to bundle her cleaning gear and vacuum cleaner over the step when–

'Nice horns.'

She'd known this sarcastic male voice since childhood. She raised her head and stared at the man, face mutinous. 'Ugh.' She stood up straight. 'What are *you* doing here?'

'Actually, I'm saving *you* from getting into trouble for interfering with a police investigation.'

'Oh? How's that?'

'Your little trip to Andrea Burdett's place.'

The collar was up on his pea coat. His facial expression was as rigid as Ellie's, and he seemed tired.

'How do you know about that?' She knew it was a stupid question as soon as it left her lips.

'Call me psychic.' Dave leant against the passenger door of his Volvo, arms crossed, one eyebrow raised. He looked irritatingly sexy. 'You were spotted by a neighbour. You do know it's a suspicious death, don't you?'

'How would I know that?'

'The crime scene tape? Forensics tent? And you couldn't stop yourself from going straight over to Andrea's...'

'*Actually*, I took Gladys some food and did her cleaning first and *then* covered Zoe's shift at the pub.' She yanked her trolley of cleaning gear. 'Could you move, please? I've got to be at the Greek restaurant in the high street by 11am, and the Christmas market is on.' Ellie rolled her trolley over the doorstep towards Dave's feet.

He sidestepped. 'So, after the pub, you used your company keys – just guessing that bit – and let yourself into Andrea's house. Am I right?'

Dave picked up Ellie's vacuum cleaner from the doorstep and carried it over to the jeep for her.

'Gotta be better than breaking in.'

'You don't deny it then?'

'Why would I do that?'

'Because you've probably broken the law.'

'I was worried about Finn. I saw him briefly at the carols and then he disappeared. I wanted to check he was OK and knew his mum had–'

'*... been murdered?*'

'I didn't know she *had* been murdered.'

Dave was right. The crime scene paraphernalia had made her wonder, and he'd confirmed it. 'That's awful. Poor Andrea.'

'Didn't it occur to you that it wasn't your job to look for Finn? That we'd need to speak to him?'

Ellie zapped the car locks with the remote. 'How is letting myself into a neighbour's house to check on her son's welfare breaking the law?' She slid the reindeer horns off her head. 'Oh, crikey. Don't tell me you're the Senior Investigating Officer?'

'Thankfully, no.' He faced her now. 'But you might end up wishing I was.'

'Doubt that very much.'

'I'm just helping Jim out. His team are low on investigators. And he was about to send a uniformed officer round to haul you in to have your prints and DNA taken.'

Ellie flinched. After the row with Andrea, if she were taken off in a police car, her neighbours would dine out on that for a month. 'Have you got all the stuff you need from Andrea's?'

'Hopefully. But no thanks to you. Our officer arrived not long after you'd been there.' He opened the boot door and placed the vacuum cleaner in the back. His phone rang. 'Sorry. Got to get this.' Walking away a little, he switched his work voice on. 'DI Blix?'

Ellie inched towards him so she could hear his conversation.

'Thallium?' Dave was quiet for a moment. 'And her stomach contents? ... OK... Cake... What sort? ... Ah. Thanks. Won't be long.'

He rang off and faced Ellie again, who had sprung away and was packing the jeep nonchalantly. 'As I was saying, we need your prints and a DNA sample. And a statement.'

Ellie didn't have to pretend not to have heard. She recalled the cake box she'd seen at Andrea's yesterday, the four plates. Her brain had spun into action, and she dashed off a text to Zoe, telling her about the cake and thallium. If only Dave had said what type of cake the police had found in Andrea's stomach.

'Er... Earth calling Ellie...'

She pressed SEND on the text.

He repeated his request.

'I'll do it as soon as I can.' She was trying to think how she could find out what sort of cake Andrea had eaten without irritating Dave further. 'I don't know if I'm coming or going at the moment. I'm two cleaners down. One's on holiday. Another's off sick. That's Zoe. I'm covering her pub shifts. Your mother appears to have moved in, which means no more Airbnb guests because she's in the spare room.'

Dave's eyebrows shot up. 'How is Zoe?'

'Why didn't you ask her when you invited her for Christmas?'

'Oh, grow up, Ellie. Is this what this is about? You're annoyed I've invited my son and daughter for Christmas Day?'

'*Our* son and daughter ... to your *new home*. While I spend Christmas with *your* mother?'

'Oh, that's what's bugging you?' He rolled his eyes. 'Look, I'm sorry about my mother. I've told her she can stay with me, but she refuses. But did you want me to sleep on a camp bed in my sister's spare room forever? Every night I either had to move the cat, fold up washing or hang the kids' stinking PE kits out the window.'

'I'm just saying. That's all.' Ellie blushed, aware how ridiculous she sounded.

'For goodness' sake. *You* said you wanted a divorce.' He threw his hands up in the air. 'Look. You and Mum are welcome to join us. I told Zoe and Simon to invite you, but they didn't think you'd want to come.'

'And you couldn't be bothered to ask me yourself?'

Dave sighed loudly. 'You told me not to contact you. You said, and I quote, "I hate you, and I never want to lay eyes on you ever again".'

'Yes, *because you cheated on me.*' An exhausted sob burst from Ellie. Embarrassed, she turned away from Dave, not wanting him to see the tears that were streaking her cheeks. Slamming the boot shut and muttering under her breath, she wiped her tears with the back of her hands and climbed into the driving seat of the jeep. She fumbled with the seat belt and started the engine, trying to think what to say.

In the rear-view mirror, she saw Dave, standing, hands back in his pockets, shaking his head and watching as she accelerated down the drive and away from him. It was hard to be sure whether his tight expression was anger ... or something else?

Chapter 9

10.45am

When Ellie reached the high street, traffic was at a standstill. She wound down the window and stuck out her head. Today was the day of the French Christmas Market, another of Little Wootton's traditions at Christmas, organised every year by Kathy from the bakery. The market was in full swing. Temporary lights were allowing cars through, and traffic had been reduced to one lane.

In the village, stalls straddled the high street pavement, selling cheese, bread, clothes, hats and gloves, wreaths and flowers, cakes and puddings. Shoppers darted here and there. 'Away in a Manger' blasted out from a cheap tannoy system. In the square ahead, children were queuing with their parents to go on the noisy mini-dodgem and a carousel ride.

Ellie pulled over by the chemist. She scrolled through her call log for Sally's number and hit dial.

Sally answered on the second ring.

'I've just bumped into Dave.'

'That was careless.'

'He was waiting for me outside my last job. Told me off for going over to Andrea's last night.'

'Oh, honey. You didn't, did you?'

'Yup.'

'After the pub?'

'And Mr Flippin DI is not impressed.'

'What did he say?'

Ellie filled her in.

'Oh, cripes.'

'I did learn a couple of things though.' She told Sally that Dave had said it was a murder case and that it had been cake poisoning.

'Blimey. We thought she'd had a heart attack or something. Poor Andrea. This is shocking.'

'There's more.' Ellie told Sally about Andrea's tumour. 'I feel bad for talking about the people she's had rows with–'

'Well, that stuff is even more relevant now we know she was killed.'

'True. Her only having a couple of years to live means two things. Either the person who killed her didn't know–'

'Or they couldn't wait.'

For a few moments, there was silence on the line.

'That's going to add another dimension to the killer's motivation.' Sally paused. 'And where on earth do you get hold of thallium? It's a bit Miss Marple.'

'No idea. But I've asked Zoe to look it up. She's much better on the internet than me.'

'Look, it's not often I'll defend him,' said Sally, 'but if she was murdered, you're probably getting off lightly with a telling off from him.' She sighed. 'Come on, Ells. You've been a cop's wife for twenty years. You know how this stuff goes.'

'But the police have been there. Got what they need.'

'Fair enough,' Sally said. 'How many more jobs have you got today? Do you want a hand?'

'I've got the Greek Taverna now, if I can get up the high street. Then at midday, I've got the Airbnb guy in Castle Street. I bet he'll get me ironing all the sheets for his Christmas guests. If you can face it, I'd love some help. It's so heavy, folding all that laundry and making the beds.'

'I've just finished my last alteration, and I'm not taking in any more until after Christmas. So, you're in luck. I'll meet you at Castle Street. Give you a hand. But I draw the line at reindeer horns.' She chortled down the phone.

Ellie whooped. 'Thank you.' Her phone beeped. 'I'm going to scoot. I've got a call coming in from Zoe. See you later.'

'I'll bring my super iron. Get it done in a flash.'

'You are a *diamond*.'

Ellie accepted Zoe's call.

'Hey Mum. Listen. Gran checked the rotas for who's been doing Andrea's cleaning. It's been Sue and Caroline, so I've had a quick chat with them both. Caroline told me that Kathy from the bakery dropped a cake off at Andrea's two days ago when she was cleaning. Andrea was out so she took it in for her. Caroline remembered because she was drooling over the cake and was dying to help herself to a bit.'

Ellie laughed. It was a running joke at Blix Blitz that Caroline was a cake fanatic. 'That must've been the box I saw.'

'Well, Gran says that if the police have been to her house like you say, they'll have taken all her cake in for tests.'

'True.'

'Anyway, Gran's got the bit between her teeth so she's going to pop in and have a chat with Kathy. See if she can find out who ordered the cake she delivered.'

'Oh. Excellent. Top marks for initiative.' Ellie laughed. 'While she's here, she might as well make herself useful. With all that social work experience, she'll be helping the police out no end.'

Ellie's attention started to wander because a police car was pulling up across the road from the chemist. And when the back door opened, a scruffy-looking Finn scrambled out.

She lowered the window and yelled, 'Hey, Finn. *Finn.*' Returning to Zoe, she said, 'Gotta go, love,' and rang off, lobbing her phone onto the car seat. Yanking the keys from the ignition, she jumped out. 'Finn, wait up. I want to talk to you.'

Finn turned towards her and his face clouded over. He darted towards an alley along the side of the hairdresser's, his long legs striding away from Ellie.

Ellie leaped into the road, determined to follow. One leg shot off in one direction, the other in another, and before she knew it, she was on her bottom on soggy snow. Yet again, Finn had appeared – and disappeared.

Chapter 10

11am

Inside the baker's, people were queuing at the counter. In front of them, freshly baked loaves of all sizes and descriptions lay on racks.

Sylvia had her shopping basket on her arm. She spotted Kathy at the sandwich counter, filling the chiller cabinet, and went over. 'Morning. Have you got an egg and cress on white?'

'Take this one.' Kathy handed her a wrapped sandwich. 'How's your head this morning?'

'I had an extra cup of tea and a couple of painkillers, and I'm fine now. It's Andrea I feel sorry for. And her poor family.'

'Oh, absolutely. It's terrible.'

Sylvia had run through how she was going to ask her about Andrea's cake, but she'd have to play it by ear.

She and Zoe didn't think for a moment that Kathy had poisoned Andrea, and she had to be careful because it wasn't really any of her business who Kathy had been delivering the cake for. 'Ellie's sent me in. Our Zoe's down in the dumps with this blasted glandular fever. One of Ellie's cleaners, Caroline, was admiring the lovely chocolate gateau that Andrea ordered the other day. She was doing Andrea's cleaning when you dropped it off.'

'That's right. They're one of our bestsellers. Andrea didn't order this one though.'

She needed to play it gently. She couldn't just say, 'Who did, then?'

'We were wondering if there was any chance of making one for Zoe? Cheer her up a bit. Ellie didn't realise you did a delivery service.'

'We've done one for ages, but it's not usually me who does it. Julia's got the flu, so I had to step in.'

'I bet it's nice to get out of the shop.'

'To be honest, I enjoy doing deliveries at this time of the year,' she chatted on, beaming. 'Everyone's houses look so pretty with all their Christmas decorations and fairy lights. Have you seen the blow-up Santa on the roof of the pub?' She laughed. 'We can definitely do a cake for Zoe. If you come over to the counter, I'll get you a price list. When do you want it for?'

Kathy put the tray of sandwiches down, and Sylvia followed her to the counter behind the till. She pulled an A4 menu out from behind a paperback book. 'Have you read this?' she asked Sylvia, pointing at it. 'We're doing it at the next book club if you want to come along.'

Sylvia saw it was *The Canterbury Murders*. 'Someone left a copy of this in the pub last night.' She chuckled. 'The TV show was one of few that my husband liked. Having been on the force himself, he avoided them. But he adored the landscape along the River Stour. The beautiful herons. The marshes.'

'It's very evocative and a great story.' Kathy's face lit up. 'So, you were married to a detective too? Like Ellie?'

'Yes. I know how hard it is, believe me.' She drew breath. 'Sorry. We were talking about cakes.'

'We do cards with them, if you'd like one. Sue wrote one for Andrea.'

Sylvia's ears pricked up.

'My husband took her order. She said something about a disagreement over the panto.'

Sue had ordered the cake? Had Sylvia heard that right? 'That was nice of her. The lady who runs the village bistro with her husband? Occasionally works for Ellie's cleaning business?'

'That's her.' Kathy pointed at the menu. 'This was the one she wanted. An old-fashioned Black Forest gateau. I make it with fresh cream and fresh cherries and lots of kirsch or brandy, whichever you prefer.'

'Kirsch, please. It looks gorgeous.' It was Zoe's cake, of course, but Sylvia was already imagining her first slice.

'They are delicious,' Kathy added. 'My Gordon loves them. I've adapted the recipe from one of my grandmother's.' A warm smile stretched over her face. 'I've got another batch to make this evening so you can have it tomorrow morning, if that works?'

'Perfect. Thank you. I'll drop in. Better get off. My daughter-in-law has left me in charge of Zoe.'

Sylvia couldn't wait to report back to Ellie. Sue had sent Andrea a cake over a disagreement. Had it been a kind gesture of apology? Or was it possible that it had been a calculated act that had killed her?

Chapter 11

11.30am

After the spat with Dave, Ellie was relieved to have some female company. The utility room at Phil Hammond's B&B was a hotbed of activity and noise. In one corner, two washing machines were spinning, and above each, a tumble dryer churned another load of white bed linen.

Ellie and Sally both stood at ironing boards. Ellie's mind was full of Andrea's murder, and it was a relief to chat to Sally about other things.

'I'm pleased Phil's out,' Sally said. 'We can have some fun.'

'O Come all Ye Faithful' came on the radio.

Sally cheered and cranked the volume up. Jets of steam sprayed onto the white material as she ran the fancy iron over a double duvet cover.

Ellie joined in with the first verse at the top of her voice. 'It feels a bit naughty, sneaking you in to help me. Reminds me of when we were at school, cobbling together a piece of homework that we'd forgotten to do.'

'Think of me as your unpaid helper.' Sally gestured to an invisible halo above her head. 'You *should* have help with these big laundry jobs. They're too much for one person.' She paused and spoke more gently. 'Is it cash flow? Is that why you won't take anyone else on?'

The mention of funds made Ellie freeze. 'It's always money. Has been since–' She stopped herself. She was bored of hearing herself witter on about how the break-up had affected her finances. 'It's my own fault. In a fit of pride, I told Dave to stick his money.'

'It's no wonder you're struggling. You're paying all the bills on a huge, open plan, draughty building, which has no insulation. Tell him you made a mistake.'

Ellie felt a lurch of anxiety. 'I might have to. If things don't change, I'm scared we're going to lose the windmill. I want Zoe and Simon to have it. To live there with their children, if they want to.'

'I understand that, but seriously, Ells, you need more staff. Especially while Zoe's off sick. Otherwise you'll end up ill yourself.' Sally folded the sheet she'd ironed. 'Couldn't Zoe get one of her mates to cover her bar shifts?

It's too much on top of all this. Both jobs involve being on your feet for hours.'

Ellie told Sally what she'd decided about getting help in the new year.

'Good. And if Sylvia stays for long, ask her to contribute to the heating.'

'She did offer. I said no.'

'Why? Look, I love you to bits, but you've got serious pride issues. Sylvia's saving money not paying her own bills. I'm not suggesting you demand that she hands over her pension, but a tenner a week wouldn't hurt.'

'I'll think about it. She does have the heating on *all the time*.' She rolled her eyes. 'Changing the subject – do you remember that time we had to cobble together Mrs Wilks' homework after the GCSE Biology field trip?'

'Oh, yes. Didn't we fall in the marsh and lose our planners?' Sally cackled. 'You, me, Dave and his mate, Bob, and Andrea, wasn't it?'

'That's right. Gosh. *Bob Campbell.* I haven't thought about him in decades.' Ellie chuckled as a memory bobbed up. 'Dave managed to rescue Bob's glasses, but that was it. None of us knew what the homework was.'

'Didn't Andrea go out with Bob for a while?'

'I think so, yeah,' said Ellie. 'Oh – and her sister from the year above went out with him too. D'you remember? Dawn, was it?'

'Debbie. I'm pretty sure she lives locally. She teaches a yoga class at the community centre in Deal. I saw her name in their catalogue a few months ago. Debbie Burdett.'

'She must know what's been going on with Andrea.' Ellie's brain slipped into its groove again. 'Actually, now you mention Bob, I'm sure Dave told me he was one of Finn's godfathers.' She removed her pullover, fanned her cheeks, then picked up another set of bed linen.

'Bob must've kept in touch with Andrea, then,' Sally said. 'He might know what things have been like for her and Finn.'

'I'll ask Zoe to see if she can track him down.'

'It's so sad what's happened. I hope the police catch her killer quickly.'

'Goodness knows how things will pan out. All the government cuts. Dave says they're really short-staffed.' Ellie's thoughts shifted from Andrea to her son, Finn. 'You know, Andrea spent a lot of her life on her own. And now Finn is on his own too.' She paused. 'What do you remember about when Andrea got pregnant? As soon as Dave proposed to me, and we had that stupid row, she stopped speaking to me. I've never really known what was going on for her after that. I think Dave knew snippets, but we didn't talk about her.'

'I heard she got together briefly with a fellow actor when she was in a West End theatre production.'

'Oh? Of course, she was an actress, wasn't she? How did I forget that? Especially as she was doing all that amateur dramatics stuff.'

'This is all second hand, you understand,' Sally told her. 'Kathy said it didn't last. Andrea got pregnant with Finn and decided to have him and be a single parent.'

Ellie told Sally about the butcher's remarks about Finn's father being absent.

'Kathy said the same: the actor chap didn't want anything to do with Andrea when she got pregnant, and nothing to do with the baby when he was born either.' Sally folded up the duvet cover, placed it in the rack and took another one from the ironing basket. 'Silent Night' was now playing, and she sang along, overemphasising the long vowels.

'It's been really tough for both of them. No wonder Finn's had issues with anger. I knew he was struggling because, every so often, Dave would rescue him when he got into a scuffle, bring him home and give him a pep talk and then drop him off at Andrea's. Then, one day, he said Finn and Andrea had had a massive bust-up, and she had kicked him out. Dave was trying to get him into a local hostel.'

'That's when he got into drugs, I gather.'

'Yep. Three-ish years ago. Something like that.'

'Can't have been easy for Andrea either.'

'In the Bleak Mid-Winter' started up. By sheer coincidence, Ellie and Sally dropped their voices to a baritone at the same time to sing one of the verses. They managed a couple of lines before they dissolved into giggles.

'This is the most fun I've ever had while doing ironing,' said Ellie. 'D'you want a job?' she joked.

Sally sniggered. 'By the way – dare I mention Dave? How are things on that front?'

'Ugh.'

'Meaning...?'

'...that I don't think I can see us ever getting back together now.' She told Sally about the new flat.

'Right. Let's break this down.'

'I knew there was a reason you're my friend.'

'So, he's moved into a flat of his own. You don't expect him to crash at his sister's forever, do you? You have a permanent home. Why shouldn't he?'

Ellie faked a sob. 'True. When you put it like that, it sounds silly. I suppose it means he's moving on. That's all. And it scares me.'

'Why? It depends what he's moving on from, surely?'

'I guess. And I have no idea. What worries me is that when we move on, we sometimes don't want to go back.'

'Maybe he's simply moved on from crashing in a single bed at his sister's. He told Pete it takes him an hour to get to the police station.' Her expression was earnest. 'Right. I've finished.' She switched her iron off. 'Do *you* want to go back?'

'To what? I don't know. Not to someone who wanted an affair. Someone who *had* an affair.'

'Look. I haven't a clue what's going on in his life so I'm simply playing devil's advocate here. But what if you could both move on – together?'

Ellie stared at her.

'Have you talked to him about it?' Sally peered at Ellie as if she was checking to see how her questions were landing. 'Did he tell you why he had the affair? That's usually the key, isn't it?'

'We haven't talked about any of it. Haven't been able to. I've felt so ruddy angry with him, all I've wanted to do is yell at him.'

Sally smiled kindly. 'Give it time.' She paused. 'Do you think he wants to get back together?'

Ellie shrugged. 'No idea. I've screamed at him so much, I think I've made him hate me.' Her face dropped.

'I doubt that. But he's an attractive guy, Ells. You know that from school. Half the girls there had a crush on him. And you know what men are like. They hate being moaned at, let alone shouted at.' She paused, adding, 'I say this as someone who loves you dearly. If you want to get back together with him, maybe try not to yell at him. Because there are plenty of non-shouty women around who'll jump at the chance of having a fella like him.'

Chapter 12

3pm

Little Wootton's village hall was one road back from the high street and doubled as the local community centre and scout hall. The large, red brick building had a slate roof and was attached to the side of St Mary's church. A huge banner hung across the front door, reading: 'WOOTTON PLAYERS: *Cinderella.*'

Ellie parked the jeep. Sally's comments about Dave had sent her into a panic. She didn't doubt that her friend had her best interests at heart, but what if he had already moved on? Started seeing someone?

Before she went in, she found Debbie's contact details on the community centre website and rang her mobile number. Debbie didn't answer so she left a message. Next, she checked her texts. There was one from Zoe:

'Update: 1) thallium readily available on the internet. Slow death over a few days. Abdominal pain. 2) Gran says Sue ordered Andrea's cake. Caroline took the delivery (from Kathy, because Julia's off with flu) when she was doing A's cleaning. Said it looked proper lush.'

Then she dialled into her voicemail. There was a message from Sylvia:

'Hi, Ellie. Zoe has gone onto Facebook from your laptop and thinks she's found Bob Campbell. You've got friends in common all round this area, apparently, including Dave. Chubby face, round glasses and a broad grin. Does that sound like him? He lives a few miles away with his wife in Farthingloe. She's sent him a friend request for you along with a private message. She says you might want to check she's got the right person and see if he replies. By the way, Zoe asked Sue about the cake delivery. What's strange is that Sue didn't mention that she had sent it to Andrea.'

Sylvia was right about Sue. There was something strange going on. They'd need to find out more.

Ellie opened Facebook on her phone. She clicked on her friend requests and saw Bob's warm face smiling at her from his profile. She'd check back later.

Ellie timed her visit to the village hall so that when she arrived, the cast of *Cinderella* wouldn't be there, just Mike and the set-building helpers and engineers. She pushed open the double doors and walked along the linoleumed corridor towards the hall. 'Hello-o,' she called out to announce her arrival.

Julia, a local teenager, popped her head out from a side room. 'Oh, hi Mrs Blix.'

Ellie did a double take. Kathy had said Julia had flu. So why was she at the hall?

Behind Julia, Ellie was surprised to see Sue, painting wallpaper for the set. She was in jeans, and had her blonde hair dragged back into a messy bun. Ellie knew Sue a bit as she sometimes took on cleaning shifts when she needed some extra money.

'How's Zoe?' Julia asked. 'We were hoping she'd be well enough to come back soon.'

Julia was younger than Zoe but they knew each other through the group. Ellie filled Julia in. 'Hopefully, it won't be long. I heard you had flu. Are you better?'

Julia's mouth fell open. 'Me? No. I'm fine.' She chatted on. 'Are you coming to see the panto? Mike and Jane have created an amazing production. Jane's rewritten parts of the script. Modernised it. The tickets have been selling like hotcakes. Well, they *were* until Mrs Bur–' She broke off abruptly, as though she realised she was being a bit tactless. 'Oh dear.' Julia lowered her voice. 'I temp at Dad's solicitors on Mondays and Tuesdays. Mrs Burdett came in a couple of weeks ago. She was really excited. Planning lots of things.'

Ellie felt a bit grubby, soaking up what Julia was saying when she knew the young woman had already said too much about her father's client, but it was impossible to stop listening.

'She said her sister was going to be annoyed, but she wanted to update her will.'

Ellie was dying to find out more when Mike appeared from the hall. He was a stout man with a beard, wearing jeans, a lumberjack shirt and khaki waistcoat with workman's pockets in it. 'Ellie. Have you come to give us a hand with painting the set?' His face was glowing.

She brandished a box of mince pies apologetically. 'I haven't, I'm afraid. But I'll happily make a cup of tea for everyone, if you fancy it?'

'Now you're talking. I haven't had any lunch.'

'How many are we?' Ellie peered through the doorway into the hall. 'Two, four, five, six. Anyone behind the scenery?'

Mike shook his head. 'We were supposed to have the dress rehearsal tonight, but with Andrea's tragic passing, we aren't going to be able to.'

'Six plus me. Let me go and make that cuppa, and we can have a chat.'

Five minutes later, Ellie was in the hall with a tray. On it were seven mugs and the mince pies. She handed a mug to Mike and took one herself. 'Show me this set then. It looks terrific.' She wanted to ask about the disagreement Sue and Andrea had over the panto. She felt uncomfortable quizzing him about it now that Andrea wasn't around anymore, but if it helped to find out who had killed her, it was probably OK. She followed Mike up onto the stage.

'Gemma has done most of the set. Isn't she talented?' He pointed to Cinderella's house. 'She's created interior walls on one side and exterior on the other. They're on a rather nifty wheelie system so we can spin them around in between the acts.' He demonstrated how it worked.

All of a sudden, Ellie was in a rural nineteenth-century French house. Stained walls, stone floors, elegant shutters.

'Thing is, I don't know if the performance *should* go ahead.' He was facing her now.

'Oh, that would be a shame. All this hard work.' Ellie gestured to the beautiful painted walls. The architecture. The furniture.

'It's also a case of whether it *can* go ahead. We've lost two days of rehearsals and last-minute tech stuff. But quite apart from the timing of things, Andrea's been such a big part of the group. It doesn't feel right without her.'

'She wouldn't want you to cancel the performance. You know that. She'd be the first to tell you to pull yourself together and say the show must go on. Have you been able to fill her part?' Ellie remembered all the framed photos of Andrea's West End plays which her cleaning staff had told her about over the years. Andrea had even done a couple on Broadway.

'Sue's agreed to step in.' Mike thumped down onto a wooden box, slopping tea over his jeans. 'We – that's Jane and I – only gave Andrea a smallish part in this one. She'd missed lots of rehearsals and, I don't know how to put this, she didn't seem herself. This was a couple of months ago when we were casting. She kept having tiffs with people, and we were worried about members leaving and it affecting the play. We're a small group. It isn't easy to replace people at short notice.'

'Of course. Thank goodness she only had a small part then.'

'In one sense, yes. But it led to a lot of bad feeling. Andrea went absolutely nuts at me about it when we told her. I honestly thought she was going to give herself a heart attack.'

'Oh dear. She has been having a few rows recently.' Ellie grimaced, because she had been one of those people. 'Did you get the impression it was just the part that was upsetting her? Or was something else worrying her, do you know?'

'Jane said something was causing Andrea immense stress. She overheard her on the phone one evening. Out the back, by her car, and she was screaming down the phone, telling the person – in very strong language – to leave her alone. She was shouting, saying the person had ruined her life. Jane was really worried. She came straight in and told me.' He rubbed his chin and top lip, then threw his hands in the air. 'What do you do in that situation, though? It's not information you've sought, but nevertheless you've heard something that wasn't meant for you.'

'Yes, quite.' Ellie was trying to think what she would have done. As a cleaner, she was regularly hearing and seeing things she didn't want to. And often felt compromised by them.

'Jane asked Andrea if she was OK when she came back into the hall, but she didn't like to ask about what she had heard because she didn't think it was her business. You know?' He took a swig of his tea. 'She regrets it now, of course. Do you think it had anything to do with why Andrea was murdered?'

Ellie was processing what Mike had divulged. Telling someone to leave her alone. Who could that be? And that they'd ruined her life. That was pretty strong. 'Golly, I don't know.'

Andrea had been an actress, and 'you've ruined my life' was a figure of speech ... but when an adult said it, it was usually over something big. She'd have to see what else she could dig up. Someone had to know if Andrea was being harassed, surely? Debbie? Martha?

'Going back to Andrea's acting,' Mike continued, 'Jane and I felt so bad that we promised to give her the lead in the Easter production.'

'Oh?'

'She told Jane she'd started on some new medication and hoped it would help with her memory. She promised she would come to every rehearsal and that she would make sure she didn't cause any ructions with the group.' Mike shook his head. 'She was so excited about it.' He covered his face with his hand. 'I feel awful now. She said the Easter play was going to be her last one. She was going to retire from the group after that, and she wanted one final chance to shine.'

'Did she tell you what the medication was for?'

'No, and Jane and I didn't want to pry. She said she had been receiving some treatment, and we left it at that.'

'Yes, it's tricky, isn't it, when it's sensitive like that?'

'Jane and I discussed it before we agreed to give her the lead for next year. We decided we would make sure we had a good understudy in case anything happened and Andrea had to pull out.' Mike smiled bravely. 'To be honest, the Easter production is the least of our worries at the moment.'

As Ellie gathered up everyone's mugs, she was still taking in what Mike had told her. Some of it fitted with what she already knew. 'Has the Easter production and cast been announced yet?' An idea was occurring to her.

'Yes. We always list our upcoming productions on our website along with who's playing the lead part. The full cast isn't announced until nearer the time.'

'Anyone know about Andrea getting the starring role?'

'Jane and I, obviously. And anyone else who's seen that page on the website.'

Ellie groaned inwardly. That meant anyone could have found out about Andrea's role, and there was no way of knowing who. 'Anyone registered any objection about the casting?' Ellie knew what am dram groups were like for rivalry and gossip.

'Not to me. Not so far, anyway. You can check with Jane.'

'Thanks. I'll have a word with her. See if she can shed any light on things.' She checked her watch. 'I've got to go. See how Zoe is. Nice to catch up. I hope you manage to open Cinderella. Lots of people are looking forward to it – including Zoe, Sylvia and me. We've booked for Christmas Eve. Perhaps we need an SOS on the Lower Wootton Facebook page. See if we can get you some help.'

A huge smile broke over Mike's face. 'Ah, Ellie. You're a star.'

'Before I go – has Julia just had flu?'

'Don't think so.' Mike pursed his lips. 'She's been here with Gemma and Sue painting the set for the last three days.'

Ellie let out a sigh. So, that was it. Julia had been bunking off work to help out with the play. Told Kathy she had flu. Thank goodness it was nothing more sinister.

As Ellie left the hall, she was trying to figure out if she'd learnt anything about who might have killed Andrea. The thing that was making her most curious was, who had Andrea been telling to leave her alone – and why? And was anyone annoyed about Andrea getting the lead in the Easter play? They knew Sue and Andrea had disagreed over the Christmas panto. Perhaps Sue had issues with the spring production too.

Ellie passed the side room on her way towards the exit. The door was ajar. She stopped. Sue was head down, still busily painting away as though her life depended on it.

She placed her paintbrush back in the pot, then took the top off a black marker pen and scribbled an instruction for the set builders, 'OTHER SIDE OUT', drawing a bubble above the 'I' – as a dot – even though it was in capitals.

Hold on. Hadn't Ellie seen that writing somewhere before? Damn. She couldn't think where. And nor could she shake the sense that Sue was deliberately keeping a low profile. She was usually sociable and chatty and hadn't joined them all for a cup of tea. Was Ellie imagining it, or was something off?

Suddenly, Sue noticed Ellie was there. She gasped and dropped the length of wallpaper. It flapped down onto the linoleum, writing upwards. 'You frightened the life out of me.' Her voice was a whisper, her face as pale as the paper.

'You OK?'

'Course...' She answered too quickly. 'Why shouldn't I be?'

Ellie smiled at her and was about to carry on walking when she remembered the envelope she'd picked up off the floor at Andrea's. That's where she recognised the writing from. It was the way Sue dotted her 'i's with a bubble rather than a dot. Sue must have left a card for Andrea with the cake. 'Caroline was drooling over the gateau you sent to Andrea. That was a lovely thing to do.'

Sue shrugged.

'When Zoe asked you about it, you didn't say anything.'

'It's personal.'

She wasn't usually this defensive.

Ellie was desperately trying to think how to phrase her question. It was obvious Sue didn't want to talk about it, but if she was annoyed with Andrea for forgetting her lines, why would she send her a cake? Ellie was going to have to embellish the truth a bit. 'Guess we've both got the police asking questions about our rows with Andrea?'

Sue looked up. 'Mike told you, then?' Her expression was pained.

'Yup.'

'I'm sure half the village are talking about me being a cow to her.'

'We all say and do things we don't mean.' Ellie paused, gathering her thoughts. 'She came round to my house wanting to talk to me and I wouldn't let her in. I reckon the village have been talking about that too. I feel dreadful.'

'I don't know *what* I feel. The cake was my husband's idea, not mine.' Sue looked perplexed. 'Now, if you don't mind, I need to get on. I've got to get back to the bistro and help Alan prep the kitchen for tonight.'

Chapter 13

3.15pm

Back in her jeep, Ellie's mind was churning with questions. Finn seemed to be behaving oddly. He kept turning up and disappearing. Then there was Andrea's will. Why had she updated it? Who was harassing her? And was Sue involved with Andrea's death, or was it just a coincidence that she was acting strangely too? Why had her husband Alan suggested sending Andrea the cake? She needed to talk to Sylvia and Zoe. See what else they'd found out. She brought up Zoe's number on her phone and dialled.

'Hey Mum.'

'Is Gran with you?'

'Yep. She's just made some flapjacks.'

'I'm going to be passing through the village in a few minutes. Could you both meet me at the pond in ten minutes? Where the heaters are.'

'Sure.'

'I know we guessed as much, but your dad has confirmed Andrea's death was murder.'

'We must find her killer then. I'll tell Gran.'

'Wrap up warm, lovey, will you? It's Baltic today. And can you bring me one of Gran's flapjacks?'

'Will do. See you there.'

Ellie rang off, switched the fan heater on and pulled her scarf up round her neck. She tore the plastic packaging off a box of champagne truffles from a customer and stuffed one in her mouth, biting into the liquid centre and relishing the sugar burst on her tongue. They were scrumptious.

Before she forgot, she went onto the village Facebook page and posted a request for volunteers for the Wootton Players. Then she checked her phone for text messages. She stopped scrolling when she saw one from Dave:

'I was about to remind you to come down to the station, but I've just had a call from Jim. They don't just need your prints and DNA. They need to question you too. So, if you don't come in, you'll be getting a visit and...'

Ellie selected the message and deleted it gleefully – and exhaled. Dave was *not* going to tell her what to do any more. Then she checked her friend requests on Facebook.

Bob had accepted and replied to her message.

'Ellie! Lovely to hear from you. I'm in Appledown today, helping with the copsing in the woods, and then cutting down two dangerous trees in Priory Park tomorrow. Give me a buzz on 07329 772900.'

A few minutes later, Ellie was back in the heart of the village. She parked at the edge of the green, got out and stepped over the small black chain fence, relieved to have thick-soled boots on. Overnight, the temperature had dropped again and the ice on the duck pond was even more opaque. The snow had crisped over, and children were skating on the pond, squealing with delight, arms moving like wings in the afternoon light while their parents stood by anxiously, hoping their offspring would stay upright.

Kathy's bakery had opened their trailer. At the main hatch, they were selling hot drinks, cakes, soup and sandwiches, and at the end of the trailer, they had a chestnut roaster.

Ellie crunched over the snow and joined Sylvia and Zoe who were sitting under one of the heaters by the pond, both with their hands around paper cups. They were watching two local children rapturously devour some roast chestnuts with their parents.

Zoe held out a cup for Ellie. 'Got you a hot chocolate.'

'Here you go.' Sylvia dropped a warm, sweet-smelling package of aluminium foil into Ellie's coat pocket. 'One piece of flapjack.'

Ellie felt a burst of appreciation for Sylvia. Her own mother was living in France with her new partner, and they hadn't met up for a couple of years.

To the right of where they were sitting, a large sandwich board was advertising Santa's Grotto. Zoe had adored this when she was a child. She was going to love taking her own children one day.

'Tom from the pub is Santa this year.' Zoe must have seen her mum looking at it.

'He's certainly got the build for it,' Sylvia said, a bit waspishly, and the three of them laughed.

'OK, team,' said Ellie. 'Let's discuss developments before we all freeze.' She briefly put on a mock-serious voice. 'I've convened the inaugural meeting of Blix Investigators because I have a number of questions.' Losing the joking tone, she continued, 'First, why does Finn keep turning up and disappearing?' She told them about the police car and the alley. 'Then there's Andrea's will. Why did she update it? And I've just found out that someone was harassing her. Who?' She watched Sylvia and Zoe's expressions. 'Finally, Sue is behaving oddly. Is it just a coincidence or could she be involved with Andrea's death? Why did Sue send Andrea a cake? Apparently, it was her husband's idea.'

'Maybe Finn is just lying low?' said Zoe. 'Avoiding anything stressful? His mum has just died. And he might be busy?'

'That's a possibility,' Ellie replied. She'd had the distinct impression he hadn't wanted to talk to her, but it could have been for the reasons Zoe suggested.

'In my experience, it's quite common for people to review their will arrangements when they know they're going to die.' Sylvia sipped her hot chocolate and tucked her scarf into her blue parka. 'They may have made their will years earlier and left it because it's a pain to alter. But death changes the reference frame. You think about the people you're leaving behind.'

'Yes, I got the sense from Andrea's email to me that she was putting all her affairs in order. She wanted to clear the air before she died.' Ellie unfolded the foil round Sylvia's flapjack and took a bite. She could see Zoe's brain ticking over.

'I googled wills,' Zoe said. 'A person's will enters the public domain after probate–'

'That's going to be too late,' Ellie cut in. 'We need to know *now* who her beneficiaries were and are.'

'Someone in her family will know.' Sylvia spoke through a mouthful of crumbs. 'Who is there, apart from Finn?'

'There's Debbie, her sister. I've contacted her. Hopefully, she'll have some information.' She took out her phone and checked her email. 'Nothing back from her yet.'

'On the subject of Sue – Kathy said the cake was something to do with a disagreement over the panto,' Sylvia said.

'I've just come from the village hall. Sue didn't want to talk about why she'd sent the cake.' Ellie relayed Sue's comments. 'Any thoughts, team?'

Sylvia cleared her throat. 'The question is – why not?'

Ellie gave the two women a summary of what she had learnt from Mike.

Sylvia raised her eyebrows. 'In that case, there are two possible explanations. The cake was a gesture of apology for being mean to Andrea–'

'...or the opposite.' Zoe's face was animated. 'She wanted to get Andrea out of the way, so she sent her a poisoned cake.'

'Except – Kathy made the cake and delivered it herself,' Sylvia said. 'When would Sue have had the chance to poison it?'

'True. Could *Kathy* have put poison in the cake?'

'The police will have taken the cake crumbs from Andrea's for testing,' Ellie replied. 'They'll know whether the poison was in that cake. If it was, they'll be interviewing Kathy for sure.'

'Whatever we think about it, Sue had a known grievance against Andrea,' said Sylvia. 'What motive could Kathy have for wanting her out of the way?'

'Can't think of anything. Can you?' Ellie had polished off the flapjack. 'That was divine,' she said to Sylvia as she brushed the crumbs off her hands. 'You should get Kathy's kiosk to sell them.' She gestured to the trailer.

'Sylvia Blix's award-winning Windmill Flapjacks.' Sylvia laughed and looked at the other two women. 'Back to Kathy for a moment.' Her tone was serious now. 'Just because we can't think of a motive for Kathy, it doesn't rule her out. She had the perfect opportunity.'

Sylvia was right.

'And what's this about someone harassing Andrea?' Sylvia added.

Ellie told them what Mike had said about the phone call.

'Could it have been Sue?' Zoe asked.

Sylvia's features folded into a frown. 'Given Sue was open about her disapproval of Andrea, why would she phone her and harass her? Surely if she had something to say, she'd say it to her face at the rehearsals?'

'That's a good point, but she might have had something to add. I guess we need to consider that it might have been someone else. It'll be interesting to see what Debbie has to say.'

'What about Martha? She was Ellie's best friend. She'd be likely to know if someone had been harassing Andrea.'

'I can't see Martha talking to me at the moment.' Ellie told them how she had been at the carols when Andrea collapsed.

'If she's annoyed with you, she won't want to talk to me.' Zoe was looking at her mum. 'I reckon you should talk to her, Gran.'

'Righto.' Sylvia's eyes danced with excitement. 'I'll get over to her place as soon as we've finished.'

'Wow.' Zoe peered at her gran. 'Get you. At this rate, we'll have solved Andrea's murder before the police do.'

'That would be good, wouldn't it? It would certainly make me feel a bit better about refusing to speak to Andrea when she came round.' Ellie paused. 'This concludes the inaugural meeting of Blix Investigators. Well done, ladies.' She got to her feet. 'I'm going to nip over to Andrea's. Dave says the police have finished there, and I want to have another go at finding Finn. If anyone's got information on Andrea, it'll be him.'

Chapter 14

4pm

Sylvia stood at Martha's front door, not knowing what to expect of the woman she'd heard people talk about. The Old Post Office was a large brick and flint house three roads away from the high street. The white shutters, which framed every window, gave it an elegant feel. She was hoping she was going to be able to talk her way in without coming across as a complete Miss Marple busybody.

'Hello. I hope you don't mind me popping round,' she said when Martha opened the door. She tried not to sound too simpering. 'I'm Zoe Blix's grandmother, and one of the ladies in the Bakery Book Group said you make the most amazing lemon meringue pie.'

Martha's eyebrows went up.

Sylvia was trying to remember not to mention Ellie. 'Our Zoe's got this beastly glandular fever, and I was hoping to make something to cheer her up on Christmas Day. You know how it is. All that turkey and gravy and greasy puddings.'

Martha was listening patiently.

'Something citrussy would be so refreshing. So, rather shamelessly, I've come to ask for your recipe. I hope that's not too cheeky.' Sylvia gathered up her bag and moved towards the open door.

'Oh. Of course. Come in.' Martha stood back and let Sylvia enter. 'It's Sylvia, isn't it?'

'That's right.'

'Go through. The kitchen's straight ahead. I use an adapted Nigella recipe.'

Sylvia was itching to ask her about Andrea straightaway. 'Thank you. Are you nearly ready for Christmas?'

Martha followed Sylvia along the hall. 'I don't really do Christmas, I'm afraid. This year is going to be even sadder than usual, unfortunately.'

'Yes, awful about Andrea. I know you were great friends.' She decided against mentioning the police in case it brought the conversation round to Ellie. 'What a gorgeous room. Such high ceilings.'

'Thank you.' Martha walked over to the worktop and picked up a thick hardback. 'This is the book. You can take a photo of the recipe if you want, on your phone.' She flicked through it and found the page. 'I use a bit more sugar than Nigella recommends, but it doesn't make much difference.' She handed it to Sylvia. 'How are you enjoying the village? You're Dave's mother, aren't you?'

'Yes, that's right. Oh, I love it. It's so friendly. And it's super to spend some time with Zoe. Help out a bit while she's ill.' Sylvia placed the cookbook on the worktop and got her phone out of her bag. 'Everyone's so stressed these days, aren't they? My son certainly is. It can really affect our health, can't it?' She felt a bit silly, waffling on, but she had to be a bit subtle.

'True. I can barely remember a time when I wasn't stressed. Perhaps before my son died, but that seems like a lifetime ago now.'

'I'm sorry to hear that.' Sylvia opened the camera on her phone and snapped an image of the recipe. 'I see Nigella makes her own pastry.' She gave a little laugh. 'Of course she does.' She rolled her eyes and put her phone back in her bag. 'Age doesn't help either, does it? My Dave, Zoe's mum, Andrea – they're all that age when heart attacks and strokes can happen.'

'True.'

'One of the book club ladies was saying the other night how stressed Andrea was before she died. That's such a shame.' Should she mention the tumour? If Martha knew about it, it could easily make her shut down. If she didn't, it might send the conversation in a different direction.

'She *was* stressed. I wish I could have done more, but she'd become a bit reluctant to let me help her in the last few months. When I asked her about it, she denied it.'

Now, this was interesting.

'Perhaps it was pride. I don't know.' Martha looked wistful.

'It's not easy when you live alone. I do, too. It's lovely to have help, but none of us wants to feel like a burden, do we?'

'Maybe that was it. Who knows?' She drew in a long breath.

Sylvia sensed the conversation was over.

Martha checked the clock on the kitchen wall. 'I need to get cracking. I've got to make a phone call.' She moved towards the door. 'Thanks for popping round. I hope Zoe enjoys the lemon meringue pie.'

Sylvia thanked her for the recipe and said goodbye. As she walked back down the path, she couldn't shake the feeling that there was a deep sadness in Martha. It wasn't surprising, of course. She had lost not just her son, but now her best friend too.

Chapter 15

4pm

When Ellie arrived at the Priest House, she half expected a police guard to be outside. But Andrea's house was in total darkness and there was no-one in sight. The porch was empty. With her dog-walking torch in her hand, she strode past the house next door and nipped along the path at the side of the building into an overgrown alley.

All Ellie could hear was her own breath. She approached the back door, opened it with her keys and entered.

Inside, she switched the lights on and Mouse rushed to greet her. The pans and dishes had been washed. The cake box had gone and the room was lived-in tidy.

'Finn? Are you here?'

The computer was off.

'Finn? It's Ellie Blix.'

The beanie was no longer beside the computer but the business cards still were. Ellie picked one up, fished her phone out of her pocket and dialled Finn's number.

Somewhere, there was a faint sound of a phone ringing.

She strained her ears. Opened the kitchen door into the hallway. 'Finn? Finn, are you up there?'

The ringing stopped.

Ellie took the carpeted stairs one step at a time, listening, looking around her. When she reached the landing, she rang the number again. She followed the ringtone to a door. 'Finn?' She knocked.

Nothing.

She pressed the handle and eased open the bedroom door. On the bed, a mobile phone was ringing and pulsating red at the edges. A long charge cable was plugged into an extension lead. Ellie swooped on the device and swiped the screen. When she saw the text messages on his lockscreen, the familiar image as his screensaver, she dropped the phone like it was a burning coal. It bounced on the duvet.

She cupped her hands over her face.

But it was too much.

Compelled to look again, she snatched the phone back up. Her daughter's face was looking back at her. On the lock screen, a recent text message was from Zoe.

'Mum's on her way over.'

Chapter 16

4.30pm

Sylvia and Zoe were in the kitchen when Ellie arrived home. Zoe was in her pyjamas. She was buttering crumpets at the worktop and had her back to the front door. Sylvia was sitting at the table, knitting.

Rebus dashed over to greet Ellie, squealing and wriggling.

Zoe turned to look at her mum. 'How did you get on?' A red blotch was creeping up her neck.

'Tell me about your relationship with Finn Burdett.' Ellie's voice was accusatory.

Sylvia looked up from her knitting.

Still in her coat, hat and boots, Ellie strode towards her daughter. Snow and mud flicked over the floor of the windmill.

'*Mum?*'

Ellie stood facing Zoe. Her features were pinched. 'I wondered why you said "who?" when I told you I'd seen Finn at the carols.' Ellie's face was deadpan. 'Is that where you went last night? To meet him?'

'I went to see if he was OK.' Zoe's cheeks momentarily drained of colour, then flushed pink again. 'How do you know?'

'I've seen his phone. It was on charge. Seen the photo of the two of you. He must not have got your message warning him I was on the way.'

Zoe rubbed her nose, seemingly unsure of what to say. 'What do you want me to tell you?'

'Is it serious?'

'Yes. We love each other.'

Ellie caught the defiance in Zoe's voice. The pride. She slid her hat off, then her coat, dumping them on the back of a chair. 'How long has it been going on?'

'A while.'

'How long?'

'Since Dad ... since last Christmas.'

Sylvia sat up at the mention of her son.

Ellie leant over, unlaced her walking boots, yanked them off and carried them over to the door.

Zoe tracked her mum's every movement.

'A year is a long time. Why didn't you tell me?'

'I was scared.'

'Of what? It's not as if you haven't had a boyfriend before.'

Zoe shrugged.

'If you were scared, what were you scared of?'

'What you'd say.'

'Why? If he loves you, what's the problem?'

Zoe shrugged again.

'Well?'

'Andrea.'

Ellie pulled out a kitchen chair and dropped down onto it. She stared at Zoe. 'What about her?'

Sylvia got up and shuffled over to the worktop. She filled the kettle and switched it on.

'She's his mum.'

'So what?'

'You and her don't speak. And–'

'That was nothing to do with you. *Or* Finn.'

'No, but... Here, do you want tea? You look cold. Let me make you a tea.' Zoe scooted over to the worktop and took two mugs from Sylvia. She reached up into the cupboard for another.

'Why did Andrea being his mum create a problem?'

'I can't tell you. I promised.'

'Heaven help me, Zoe. What's going on? Why can't you tell me? Promised who?'

'Dad.' Zoe's face puckered, as though saying his name cut at her throat.

Sylvia seemed to brace herself.

'Your dad knows?' Ellie unwrapped her scarf. Pulled her thick jumper off.

'He made me promise not to tell you.'

'Why?'

'He thought... We *both* thought it might make you, I don't know, take against Finn ... or something.'

'Because she and I fell out in sixth form?'

'Because it was over Dad. And...'

'It was. But it was twenty-five years ago, for goodness' sake. I don't get it.'

'Ask Dad.'

'Ask him what? What has you seeing Finn got to do with–?' Ellie got up. 'Wait.'

She paced across the kitchen to the window, wiping condensation from the glass. From the second floor of the windmill, lights twinkled over the snowy fields down to the sea.

Suddenly, it all made sense. Zoe's secrecy. And why she was suggesting that Ellie talk to Dave.

Ellie spun round to face Zoe. The full impact of what she'd realised gripped her. '*Andrea's* the woman your dad had an affair with, isn't she?'

'Good God. Is she?' Sylvia stared at Zoe.

'Speak to Dad.'

'I don't want to speak to him. I'm asking you. You've been keeping his dirty little secret for him.' She strode across the room to the sink, angrily wiping tears from her cheeks. Taking a glass from the side, she filled it and drained the whole thing, ashamed of her unkindness to Zoe. She wiped her mouth on the back of her hand. 'I remember our engagement party. Everyone was pleased for us apart from Andrea. I'll never forget her face. I know everything always feels like the end of the world when you're a teenager, but this was different. Her face was one of utter devastation. It was as though I had taken something she believed was hers.' Ellie rested against the worktop. 'How could you?' She stared at Zoe, who was shaking her head and looking down. 'You know more than anyone how much I loved him. How much I *still...*' Her words petered out.

'Mum, don't. Please.' She reached for her mother, but Ellie yanked her arm away.

'Maybe that's what Andrea wanted to tell me?'

Zoe was still shaking her head.

'...that *she* was the other woman.'

'Just talk to Dad. I have no idea what she wanted to tell you. And I'm really sorry I didn't say about Finn. It's all a mess. It seemed... I don't know ... for the best not to tell you. About her – *and* Finn.'

'You know, when I was at Andrea's the first time, she had an email up on her computer. It was an unsent one to me, begging me to reconsider and talk to her.'

Zoe opened her mouth and closed it again, as if she was about to say something and changed her mind.

'In it, Andrea said that what she wanted to tell me wasn't just about her and me. That other people are involved too.'

'You've got to talk to Dad. He knows. He'll tell you.'

'I will.' She grabbed up her car keys.

Sylvia gasped. 'Oh, Ellie.'

'Get Finn over here,' Ellie barked at Zoe. 'I want to talk to the two of you when I come back.'

Chapter 17

6pm

Dave's flat was on the ground floor of a double-fronted, detached house with bay windows, in the road that ran parallel to the high street. A black-and-white tiled path led up to the front door, over which a white rose climbed. A slate sign told her the house was called Goose Meadow.

Ellie jabbed at the doorbell and waited.

Dave opened the door in jeans and a white t-shirt. Bedhead hair, shift worker stubble. 'So glad I haven't just come off nights.' His words were thick with sarcasm.

Ellie barged past him.

'Don't mind me.' He closed the door with a weary groan. 'Straight ahead, first on the right.'

The lounge had high ceilings, freshly painted white walls, new IKEA furniture in shop-coordinated greys.

Ellie stood by the fireplace. In the wrought iron grate, amongst the white ash, a handful of orange embers glowed. On the mantelpiece, a cream hair scrunchie was tangled with dark hairs.

'Have you got company?'

Dave leant against the sofa arm and rolled his eyes. He traced Ellie's gaze to the mantelpiece. 'Don't be absurd. I got home from a crime scene an hour ago. Just got into bed for an early night when Zoe called to say you were–'

'Of course.' She dragged out the vowels. 'She called to warn you.'

Dave let out a loud groan. 'Look. Do you want some coffee? Or if you want to scream at me, would you like to get it over with?'

'What I *want*...,' she flicked the scrunchie off the mantelpiece into the basket of kindling, '...is answers.'

Dave got to his feet, glowering at her. He picked the scrunchie out of the basket and placed it back on the mantelpiece. He walked towards her, his face stitched with pain, his hands out in front of him, eyes pleading with her. 'Please. *Please* can we not do this?'

Ellie raised her palm at him in a 'stop' sign. She was shaking her head, tears streaming down her cheeks.

'Ellie, I'm sorry.' His chin was quivering. 'I'm sorry I didn't tell you that Andrea was–'

'...the woman you cheated on me with?' She was swallowing hard. 'The woman who broke up our marriage? Our home? Our–' She spluttered. 'Our *life together*?' She covered her face with her hand, trembling.

'Ellie...' Dave paused.

'And that Zoe and *her son* have been in a relationship for a year?'

Dave heaved in a massive breath. 'The two things are separate. Can we please leave Zoe out of this? None of this is her fault.' He got up and walked towards the door. Then changed his mind and faced Ellie. 'I'm going to put the kettle on. Can we talk in the kitchen? It's warmer. And given you look like you could cheerfully clobber me...' he pointed at the fire tools, '...I'll feel safer away from that poker.'

The kitchen was a mass of new IKEA cabinets and furniture in the same greys as the rest of the flat.

Ellie took the steaming mug from Dave and raised it to sip from. 'Is Zoe safe with Finn? Will he look after her?'

'I think so. He cares about her. I'm certain of that.'

'When did your affair with Andrea begin?'

Dave's face was pained. 'Do you really want to go into that?'

'Yes. I do.'

‘Why?’ He plonked down on a bar stool next to her. Placed his phone on the worktop next to him.

‘I want to know how long it went on for.’

‘Not very long. She wanted it to continue. I didn’t.’

‘Why not?’

‘Because...’ He broke off.

‘I’m waiting.’

‘Because I realised that starting something with her was a mistake.’

‘In what way?’

‘I’ve never stopped loving you.’

‘Oh, please.’ Ellie snorted. ‘You loved me ... so you started a relationship with someone else?’ Her words were loaded with pain.

‘It wasn’t like that.’

‘Says every cheating husband in the world.’

Dave sighed with exasperation. He got off his stool and wandered across the kitchen. ‘It may be what every cheating husband says. But, in this instance, it also happens to be true. It was *not* the way you make it sound.’ He turned to face her. ‘And I stopped it.’

‘*How* was I making it sound?’ She stared at him, eyes blazing, challenging him. ‘Actually, while we are at it, why did you start it in the first place? That’s what I really want to know.’

'If I tell you, you won't believe me.'

'Don't put the responsibility on me.'

He shrugged.

'Try me. Go on. Put me out of my misery.'

At that moment, his phone began to vibrate on the worktop.

Irritated, Ellie leaned over to see who was calling. The display showed one word.

RUBY.

She scowled across at Dave. 'Who is *Ruby*?'

Dave left his phone on the counter. His mouth was playing with movements. Ellie could see him thinking. She was racking her brain for times he'd mentioned a 'Ruby' at work. Maybe this was it. She was his new girlfriend.

'Oh no. You don't get to ask that.' He kept his voice soft but the tone was unmistakeable. 'You charge in here. You flick Zoe's new scrunchie into the log basket and–'

'I've never seen her wear a scrunchie.' Ellie shrugged defiantly.

'Finn bought it for her.' Still he left the phone where it was. 'No, Ellie. You kicked me out. You said you wanted a divorce. You told me you never wanted to see me again. And now you expect to know who's calling me.'

'So, this is it between you and me? This is really it?' Ellie felt tears ready to burst.

It was Dave's turn to shrug now. 'Looks like it, doesn't it?' He crossed his arms. 'Now, if you don't mind, I'd like to get back to bed. I'm shattered.'

Chapter 18

7pm

Ellie shut the jeep door and an almighty scream burst from her lungs. Her legs jiggled up and down, and she pummelled the steering wheel. Then the tears came. To start with, a sniffle, the odd tear on her cheeks, but quickly her body was shaking, her chest racked with sobs.

Eventually, she drove home in a daze, tears streaking her cheeks still. Her mind felt jangly and agitated, and her body ached. She hadn't been in close proximity with Dave for a year, and it bothered her much more than she wanted it to. Being in a home with him somehow made her long for him all the more. She'd been bothered by his familiar smell. By memories of their shared life. From family holidays to pulling his socks from the washing machine. What had gone wrong? Had they drifted apart?

Worst of all – she had blown the chance to find out why he had had the affair and how he felt about her now. All she could think about was – who on earth was Ruby?

She arrived home fifteen minutes later. All she wanted was to climb into bed, to pull the covers around her and to hide until the morning.

But when she rounded the corner, a flashy, black BMW motorbike was parked at the bottom of the drive. The rider wore a metallic helmet and full leathers. A compact figure, taller than Ellie.

Who on earth was it?

Ellie glanced up at the windmill to see if anyone had heard her come home. Sylvia was at the second-floor window, watching down.

The rider dismounted and began walking towards the jeep.

Ellie froze. Who was this, turning up at her home? The rider pulled their helmet off, and bobbed blonde curls fell over a familiar, friendly face.

'Debbie. Oh my gosh.' Ellie patted her chest. She got out of the jeep and stepped onto the pavement.

On the street, the two women stared at each other for a moment.

'I wondered who it was,' said Ellie. A wave of exhaustion swept over her and she swayed on her feet. She leant against the vehicle door to steady herself. 'You've barely changed at all though.'

After the row with Dave, it wasn't easy to switch focus, but Ellie was suddenly back at school sports day in the sweltering heat. She, Andrea, Debbie and Dave were fourteen and all doing the relay.

Debbie grinned. 'Must be all the years of yoga.'

'I should try your class. These days, my back only stops aching to let my legs take over.' She forced a laugh and wiped the last of her tears from her face, hoping Debbie wouldn't notice. It was rubbish circumstances, but it was genuinely nice to see her. 'This beauty yours? Wouldn't have put you down as a biker.' She gestured to the gleaming black motorbike.

'It is. Although not for much longer. My husband was into bikes when we met, and he made sure I got the bug.' She rolled her eyes jokingly. 'But he's been made redundant, and we can't live off what I earn from my yoga classes, so we're going to have to sell both the bikes.' Then she changed the subject. 'I got your message. I'm glad you called. I wanted to get in touch but wasn't sure if it would be welcome. I was out for a ride and I thought I'd pop by.'

'I'm really sorry about Andrea. How are you?'

'Thank you. It's been a terrible shock. Especially now they've confirmed they're investigating it as a murder.' Debbie was shaking her head in disbelief.

'Yes, I thought she'd had a heart attack or a stroke.'

'So did my husband and I.' Debbie gestured to the windmill. 'I'd forgotten you live here. Such a stunning building. We often have it as a landmark when we're out riding.'

'Thank you. We love it. It's been in my family for generations. Back to my great-grandmother's days when they used to mill flour. I grew up here. My son and daughter did too. Zoe still lives here.' Ellie felt for her keys for a moment and decided against inviting Debbie in. 'Shall we nip to the pub?' She was still taking in the day's events. 'I've had a shocker of a day and could do with a glass of wine.'

'Thought you were a bit peaky.'

'I'll explain in a sec.' Ellie took out her phone. 'I'll just send Zoe a quick text so she and her gran know where I am.' She pointed up at Sylvia in the window of the windmill. Once the text was sent, she dropped her phone back in her pocket. 'Let's go this way.' Ellie steered Debbie away from the crime scene tape and forensics tent.

'It's OK. Ben and I – that's my husband – we came here earlier. I wanted to see where she died.'

'Were you at Andrea's place after the carols?' Ellie was remembering back. 'I heard a door slam and a motorbike drove off.'

'Wasn't me.'

It must have been Finn then.

'We went to the house after coming here to the green.'

The two women clomped over the snow.

'What did the police have to say?' Ellie pushed the pub front door open, and Debbie followed her in. Jolly carols danced in the warm air. Ellie was turning questions over in her mind, but wanted to see if Andrea's sister volunteered any information first.

'They told us that she had lots of cake in her stomach – which makes sense. She'd been for a cream tea earlier in the day, I gather, and had a chocolate gateau at the house.' Debbie's face was incredulous as she mentioned the thallium to Ellie.

Ellie didn't want to admit she'd eavesdropped on Dave's phone call, so she let Debbie's comment drift and ordered their drinks at the bar.

'And – she'd been icing her Christmas cake. Ben, Finn and I were supposed to be going over there for Christmas day. And knowing Andrea, she'd probably sampled it.' She looked wistful. 'The police don't seem to know who administered the thallium.'

'Not yet.' Ellie paid for their drinks and led Debbie over to a table in the corner by the toilets where there weren't any speakers. 'I gather you've seen Finn.'

Debbie stiffened. 'Yes, he got back to his mum's a couple of days ago. Goodness knows how long for.' She rolled her eyes. 'He's been living in a shared house in Dover for three years, training as a gardener.'

Ellie mentioned that Zoe and Finn were in a relationship in case Debbie didn't know. 'Only found out about that today. They've kept it quiet for a year.'

'Crikey. Is it as long as that? Hadn't realised you didn't know.' Debbie pulled an empathetic face. 'If it's…' She broke off, because Sylvia was approaching their table with a glass of wine in her hand.

'Sylvia.' Ellie pretended to be surprised to see her. 'Would you like to join us?'

Ellie was exhausted and knew she would forget details of her conversation with Debbie, so she had asked Zoe to get her gran to come over and join them in the pub. Ellie introduced the two women and budged up on the bench so there was space for Sylvia next to her. She turned her attention back to Debbie. 'You were talking about Finn and Zoe?'

'Yes, I didn't realise you didn't know they were going out together. If it's any consolation, they seem very much in love... Although...' she hesitated, 'I'm not sure I'd want *my*...' Debbie's words petered out and a nervous look spread over her features.

Ellie couldn't help feeling that there was something specific that Debbie wanted to say about her nephew. She didn't seem keen on him at all. 'Was Andrea pleased to see him home?'

'She was.' There was reservation in Debbie's voice and a frown flickered over her face. 'But their relationship had been strained for so long, she was worried how Finn would be with her and whether there would be enough time to sort things out. Their differences weren't trivial. They weren't about a row or silly misunderstanding.'

'What were they about?'

'Finn has never been a ... a *straightforward* young man.'

Sylvia grunted quietly.

Ellie wasn't sure if Debbie had noticed. This was a different take on Finn. Several people had mentioned his anger. And, given the circumstances, it was understandable. But this sounded different.

'What do you mean, not straightforward?'

'I was wondering that,' Sylvia said.

Debbie tapped at her glass while she collected her thoughts. 'What's the best way of putting it? He's unpredictable. No, not that exactly.' She seemed to be choosing her words. 'I'm sure it was part of their specific relationship – I don't want to alarm you – but he would get so angry sometimes, it scared Andrea.'

Ellie's thoughts ran to Zoe. 'That's worrying. I'll have to have a word with him.' She took another sip of wine and tried to connect with how Debbie's information was making her feel. 'Was he always like that?'

'No. As a boy, he was adorable. Andrea was a great mum. I went to the beach with them, to Dreamland at Margate, to see Santa Claus at Deal Castle. They had a lot of fun together. I used to babysit him. He was a lovely boy.' Debbie was playing nervously with her fingers. 'But something changed when he got into his teens and started asking questions about his father.'

Ellie had heard about this sort of thing.

'It's very common in children who have a parent who's been absent all their life.' Sylvia spoke knowledgeably. 'When children hit their teens, it's all about identity, so who their parents are is extremely important.'

'Sylvia's an ex-social worker,' Ellie explained to Debbie.

'Ah, well, this'll make sense to you then. Finn went from being a loving boy to a very angry young man.'

Debbie's expression roused Ellie's suspicions. 'You aren't suggesting that he could have killed his mother, are you?'

Debbie frowned, and her delayed answer sent a cold shiver over Ellie. 'I don't think I'd go that far.' She paused.

Ellie felt Sylvia flinch next to her.

Debbie hadn't said no. This was extremely worrying.

'But you never know,' Debbie continued. 'You've only got to look at what we see on the news. People can crack at any moment, and often it emerges that they've got histories of anger and violence. Of social alienation.'

'It's true, sadly.' Sylvia's voice was resigned.

'Oh golly.' It was undeniable that some of that applied to Finn, but Debbie's comments made Ellie uneasy. She'd have to talk to Dave about it. Get his view. He knew Finn better than she did. Make sure Zoe was safe.

'I discovered something else today. Andrea was the person Dave had his affair with. I've just been to Dave's to ask him about it.' A painful sigh burst from Ellie's mouth.

Next to her, Sylvia stiffened.

Suddenly, Ellie wished that she smoked. Or that she'd ordered a quadruple gin and tonic. 'I won't ask if you knew, and please, neither of you feel you have to comment. It's awkward for everyone.'

Debbie pointed at Ellie's glass. 'I can see why you suggested the wine.'

Ellie groaned. 'The affair was bad enough because it broke us up. But knowing it was with Andrea makes it much worse somehow. Makes the betrayal even greater, or something like that.' She swallowed hard. 'But – that's for us to sort out. Apologies if it's a bit of an insensitive thing to say given what's–'

'Not at all. I have just arrived on your doorstep.'

'Andrea and I haven't talked for years, but I'm very sad about her death.'

'It's OK, I know. You two were close for a long time at school.'

Ellie realised this was the topic she wanted to ask about. 'Do you have any idea who might be behind her death? Did anyone have a grudge against her?'

Debbie was shaking her head. 'I'm sure you know: she'd fallen out with a few people over the years – and recently, too. But it's hard to imagine anyone actually wanting her out of the way *permanently*, if you know what I mean. She wasn't a bad person.'

She swiped the screen on her phone and showed Ellie a photo of Andrea and herself, hiking together along the chalk cliffs at Dover.

Ellie was pleased to listen, to not have to ask questions and think.

'My sister loved living here and had a lot of friends. Some from school, people in the village. Acting friends visited her from all over the world. And even though she had spells acting abroad, Lower Wootton was always her home.' She paused and Ellie waited while she gathered her thoughts. 'I never got the impression that your fallout bothered her on a day-to-day basis, if you know what I mean. Did it you?'

'Yes and no. I have a really busy life. The kids. The cleaning company. The Airbnb. Dave's job – when we were together. I just got on with it all. But, because we all live so close, there was a constant reminder that Andrea and I didn't talk. She requested that I did not do her cleaning, so I made sure it didn't happen. And I did things she wasn't involved with.'

Ellie was feeling her way back into how life had been over the years. 'We were both in the church choir, but that felt OK, as there are so many of us and we sing different parts.' She paused. 'But I suspect it was different for me. Dave and I got engaged when we were in the sixth form. Got married at twenty. Had Zoe and Simon. I often wondered how Andrea felt, living so close to us; so close to the man she'd apparently continued to love...' Ellie broke off. She bit back tears and took a slug of wine. Had Andrea been yearning for Dave all that time? Had she been waiting for a chance to start an affair with him?

'Oh, Ellie.' Debbie covered her mouth.

Sylvia put her arm round Ellie's shoulders and pulled her closer.

Ellie sniffed and waved her hands about. 'Sorry.'

'Shall I get you another wine?' Debbie stared at her, helpless. 'Do you want a hug?'

The two of them laughed.

'You and Dave will sort things out. I'm certain of it.'

'I'm not so sure.' She thought of the phone call. Ruby. 'I think he's started seeing someone else.'

Sylvia tutted. 'I could clip his ears.'

'If he has – it could be temporary.' Debbie shrugged. 'You two have thirty years of history, don't forget.' She recalibrated. 'I'm not making excuses for my sister, but it must've been agony for her, seeing you guys together and happy. We all saw at school how besotted he was with you. She never stood a chance really and she knew it.' Debbie's attention seemed to drift momentarily. 'It's a shame she wasn't able to move on. Find someone else and get married.'

'It really was.' Ellie's eyes met Debbie's. 'I'm not sure I can talk about it kindly at the moment. I'm furious with her.' She stopped. '*And* him.'

Debbie's face was full of sympathy.

'But we are all still alive and Andrea isn't. And it's desperately sad. Sylvia, Zoe and I are determined to help find out what's happened to her. It's the only way I feel I can help at the moment.'

Gratitude flitted over Debbie's face. 'Oh. Thank you. That's kind. I don't know how long Finn'll hang around for, of course. Probably until the will's been read.'

Sylvia grunted. 'That seems harsh, Debbie.'

It was the second time Debbie had mentioned Finn not staying around.

'I hope for Zoe's sake he's not thinking about doing a disappearing act.' Ellie pictured Zoe's face when she talked about Finn. The love that oozed out of her. For a moment, she felt scared for her daughter. Protective.

'Oh, no, no. Sorry, I didn't mean... I don't... That was thoughtless.' Debbie's cheeks flushed red.

It was obvious that she didn't hold Finn in high regard. Was it possible that he *was* after his mother's money? Andrea had updated her will, after all.

'Don't worry.' Ellie tried to push Debbie's comments out of her mind and remember what else she wanted to ask. Jane and am dram. That was it. 'One of the locals overheard Andrea screaming down the phone at someone to leave her alone. She accused the person of "ruining her life". Does that ring any bells?'

After Debbie's comments, Ellie found herself wondering – could *Finn* have been harassing his mother from his shared house in Dover?

'Oh, goodness. That sounds awful.' Debbie recoiled. 'I honestly don't know any more than I've told you.' She seemed to think carefully about what she wanted to say. 'You probably don't know this, but very early into her acting career, my sister acquired a stalker.'

'Oh heavens.'

'He was a fan, a man called Brian Silk, who was obsessed with her. He came to all her plays when she was on in the West End. Hung around the stage door. Kept turning up at cast drinks, sending her flowers. The works.'

'Did she get the police involved?'

'Oh, yes. Had to.'

'Is he still bothering her?'

'He hasn't for a long time as he's been in prison. But he's recently been released and I think might have started to contact her again.'

'Oh no.' Ellie noted his name.

'I'll have a dig around,' Sylvia said. 'See what I can find out about him. I might know his probation officer.'

'I would have thought he was the most likely candidate,' Debbie said. 'Wouldn't you?'

'Hmm. Anyone else bothering her?' Ellie wasn't finished.

'Someone in her am dram group was miffed that she'd been given a big part for the spring production.'

Ellie felt her breathing lengthen. Thank goodness Debbie hadn't mentioned Finn. 'Did she say who it was?'

'Sue Someone?'

'Sue Patterson,' Ellie replied. 'She and her husband run the local bistro. She's the lady who sent the chocolate gateau to Andrea.'

'How strange,' Debbie said.

'Isn't it?'

'She was pretty unkind to my sister. This was several months ago. Said her acting days were over and that she wasn't up to learning lines any more. She lashed out one day, calling Andrea a bad mother.'

'Oh dear. That must've been terribly upsetting.'

'It was. The comments about her memory were bad enough, but the others – she was devastated.'

'Did Sue say all this privately or in front of the group?'

'Andrea didn't say. But I gather she kept on at the group organisers, and they made her Andrea's understudy.'

'That's a strange decision,' said Ellie. 'And can't have made things easier between the two of them.'

'Exactly.'

'That's two people, potentially. Can you think if Andrea *said* who was harassing her?'

'Um, I can't remember if she said. Until recently, when she talked about it, I just assumed it was the stalker. Martha probably knows more about it. Have you talked to her?'

'Not yet.' Ellie filled Debbie in on how Martha had been on the village green.

'Oh, she'll get over it. She was probably just worried. She's always been very protective of my sister. They've known each other for years.' Debbie laughed softly. 'On occasion, I've felt a bit jealous, but Ben and I are busy, and she and Martha were so tight, I was pleased they had each other. Relieved someone had her back.'

Sylvia moved the discussion on. 'What's the situation with Finn's dad?'

'Luke.' Martha sucked in her breath. 'It's all very sad. When Andrea got pregnant, she knew they wouldn't make it as a couple, but she wanted him to be a father to Finn. He refused. Told her if she wanted to have the baby, she was on her own. Didn't give her any financial support either. Literally not a penny. And refused to have *any* contact with Finn.' She exhaled loudly.

This confirmed what the butcher had told Ellie. Sylvia was shaking her head disapprovingly.

'It's why Finn has been so angry with her. He says he didn't ask to be born, and when he was, it was into half a family.'

'Ouch. That's harsh for both of them.'

'A natural thing to feel though,' Sylvia added.

Debbie was nodding. 'Incredibly hard for Finn, and he made sure that my sister felt permanently guilty about it.'

Ellie noted another dig at Finn. She drained the last of her wine glass.

'Andrea got in touch with Luke a few months ago when she got the cancer diagnosis.'

'D'you mean her tumour?' Sylvia asked.

Debbie nodded.

'Poor Andrea. I did hear about this.' Ellie clamped her hands over her cheeks. 'I'm so sorry.'

'Thanks. She told Luke about the tumour and that she was dying, and asked him to reconsider having contact with Finn. She also asked him to include Finn in his will.'

'What was his reaction?'

'I gather he didn't want to do either, and they had a huge row. He refused to believe that Finn *wanted* to have contact.'

'Wow. I'm sure it's a complex situation, but that seems pretty callous. And strange to make assumptions about what Finn wanted.'

'Quite. This time, though, she wasn't prepared to let him off the hook. She said he owed Finn the chance to meet him and get to know his father.'

'Good for her,' said Sylvia emphatically. 'What did he say?'

'Still wouldn't do it. As far as I know, that's where things stand.'

'Dear oh dear.' Sylvia grimaced.

'But Andrea had got the bit between her teeth, and she could be very stubborn when she wanted.' Debbie took in the image on her phone again. 'She wasn't prepared to let him off the hook.'

Ellie was sifting through her memory. 'I heard he's an actor.'

'Yes. And *very* successful.' Debbie rolled her eyes. 'With a lovely wife and family who don't know anything about Finn, I gather. He's got a mansion near Canterbury, a townhouse in London and a Tuscan villa.'

'Very nice.' Ellie couldn't contain her sarcasm.

'Not short of a bob or two then?' Sylvia muttered under her breath. 'These men who refuse to pay for their children. They make my blood boil.'

'Exactly.'

'This is going to be tough for Finn.' It occurred to Ellie that, if Andrea was asking Luke to include his son in his will, Luke and his family might also have a motive for disposing of Andrea. 'Are the police speaking to him too?'

'I assume so. They asked me about him. I told them what I've told you. He can't be hard to track down. He's on the telly every week.'

'Wait a minute.' Suddenly, pennies began dropping, and Ellie realised who Finn's father was. 'He's not Luke McKenzie, is he?' Ellie asked. 'From that detective programme on the BBC?'

'That's him. He was a pathologist for a couple of years in the Scandi drama on Channel 4. Now he's the lead detective in *The Canterbury Murders*.'

'Hold on a second.' Sylvia's tone was strident. 'Luke McKenzie is a household name. Surely a TV actor isn't going to get someone bumped off? If something threatened his reputation, his career would be over.'

'I suppose it would depend on how pressing the motive was,' Ellie countered.

'And how desperate he felt?' Sylvia was tapping her chin. 'Yes, that works.'

Something occurred to Ellie. 'Does Finn know who his dad is?'

'I don't know. Andrea promised to tell him when he came home for Christmas. But whether she did or not...'

Ellie would ask Finn. Suddenly, she remembered the paperback she'd seen in the pub. What a strange coincidence. Kathy's book group was reading *The Canterbury Murders*.

She fiddle with her wine glass.

Perhaps it was just because the series was on TV?

Her thoughts shifted to what Julia had said at the hall about Andrea making plans and visiting her father's solicitor's. 'Apologies if this is a bit nosey. Do you know who Andrea's beneficiaries are? Did she have a will?'

'I don't know that either, I'm afraid. She's never talked about it. I don't even know if she had one.' Debbie paused and drew breath.

Ellie wasn't sure whether to mention what Julia had said about Andrea having been into her father's solicitors to update her will. It sounded gossipy.

'We discussed her funeral arrangements. She wanted a cremation. That's the main thing for now. I'll have a hunt through her stuff. See if I can find a will.'

'Of course.' Ellie suddenly felt exhausted. She sensed that Debbie was tired too. There were a couple of final questions she wanted to ask. 'Did Andrea tell you how long the doctors had given her?'

'Couple of years, I think.'

'In that case, for someone to kill Andrea when she was going to die soon anyway, something must've happened.'

Sylvia was nodding as she spoke, as though ideas were falling into place.

'That's exactly what I was thinking,' said Ellie. 'It's got to have been someone who – for whatever reason – couldn't wait for her to die naturally.'

Chapter 19

8pm

Ellie said goodbye to Debbie. Sylvia was tired, so Ellie sent her home and said she'd pick up a takeaway for everyone. Zoe had arranged for Finn to come over to the windmill at 9pm so they could all chat.

Ellie left the pub hankering for a curry, but The Raj was heaving so she joined the queue at the fish and chip shop instead. She was exhausted, and after the glass of wine she'd had in the pub, her stomach was reminding her she hadn't eaten for hours. As she stood, her mind was whirring from all the conversations she'd had during the course of the day. With Zoe, Dave and now Andrea's sister. Debbie's words kept darting through Ellie's mind. Her expressions lingered. From how the conversation had gone, Ellie wasn't sure whether she'd been looking at normal sisterly grief or whether there was more to

Debbie's reactions. They needed Finn's input. She had a *lot* of questions to ask him.

Ellie had her head down and was concentrating on her phone, googling Brian Silk and Luke McKenzie. She found the original court report of Silk stalking Andrea. Hopefully, Sylvia would find out a bit more about that.

Then there was Luke McKenzie.

She clicked on a couple of video clips of him. He was certainly handsome and had the sort of air that many women found attractive. Tall, confident, smart, funny, charismatic and wealthy. She was jotting notes into an app, knowing that in the morning she'd have forgotten the things that had occurred to her. How could she find out who Andrea's beneficiaries were?

And then there was Finn himself. Quite apart from his relationship with Zoe, it was worrying that his mother had been scared of him, that Debbie seemed against him and wasn't able to rule out him potentially having killed his mother. Hopefully, this, too, was natural sisterly protectiveness. Because the alternative was unbearable, especially since Zoe was in love with Finn. Surely, he couldn't have been involved in his mum's death? Could he? The conversation she was about to have with him and Zoe was going to be critical.

Gemma was in the queue behind Ellie, chatting to her friend about the Christmas panto. It was a popular event every year, and all the villagers were wondering what was going to happen. From the sound of their voices, and the recurrent giggling, they'd both been drinking.

'They've given her part...' Gemma hiccupped, '...to Sue, so, technically...' she hiccupped again, '... we should be able to go ahead with...' another hiccup, '...the dress rehearsal.'

Ellie heard a fizzy drink bottle being opened. She carried on adding ideas to her notes. If her fish and chips didn't come soon, she was going to collapse.

'Makes sense,' said Gemma's friend, Roxie. 'She *was* the understudy.'

'You say that, right?' Gemma lowered her voice without realising it was still audible to the whole shop. 'But what about that massive row they had a few months ago about the panto? Sue wasn't just going on about Andrea's acting capa... papabilitees...' she stumbled over the word, burped and giggled.

Roxie shushed her friend, making Ellie tune in, her curiosity aroused.

'Yeah,' Gemma continued, ignoring her friend. 'They were arguing in the – *hic* – kitchen at the hall and – *hic* – Sue followed Andrea into the toilets. She – *hic* – called Andrea a selfish woman and a – *hic* – bad mother.'

Roxie drew a sharp breath. 'Oh my goodness. That's so extra.'

Ellie held her breath for a few moments, absorbing what she'd just heard. It suggested there was much more to Sue's bad feeling towards Andrea than just sour grapes about an amateur dramatics part. Had the chocolate gateau perhaps been an attempt to cover up her hostility or to make out they'd resolved it? Was whatever was eating Sue enough to make her want to kill Andrea?

Chapter 20

9pm

Fifteen minutes later, Ellie, Zoe and Finn were in the lounge at the windmill, polishing off the fish and chips that Ellie had bought for them. Sylvia had got a second wind and was making tea for everyone in the kitchen.

Ellie was in a squishy armchair, and Zoe and Finn sat together on one of the sofas. She piled her greasy wrapper on the tray on the coffee table next to Finn and Zoe's and checked the notes in her phone. She addressed Finn. 'I'm afraid I have a ton of questions. Some are about your mum and some are about your relationship with Zoe.'

'That's fine. I'm so pleased you guys have been trying to find Mum's killer. I'll help any way I can. The police don't seem to have a clue.'

'Brilliant. There are gaps that we need you to fill in.'

'Ask away.'

'Let's start with why you came back to your mum's. Debbie said you've been living in Dover?' Despite her list of questions, she was having trouble knowing which were most pressing.

'Mum asked me to come home. I was pretty dubious, I've got to admit. But she said she had something important to tell me, and that she wanted us to put the past behind us.'

Ellie and Zoe caught each other's eye.

'A few months ago, she found out she had cancer and was terminally ill. She wanted to make peace before she died.'

'I'm so sorry. Debbie mentioned your mum's tumour. It must've been very frightening for her.' Ellie remembered how grey Andrea had seemed on the ground at the carols. 'Did anyone else know?'

'Uncle Bob, Auntie Debbie, Martha.' He paused and seemed nervous. 'And um ... your husband. Mum said she'd told him.'

Ellie gasped. She wanted to say, 'Why him? He's not my husband any more,' but she didn't want to make the terrible news about her. Finn was in contact with his godfather and aunt. That was good. 'Did you and your mum have time to talk? To sort anything out?' She remembered what Debbie had said about their differences being deep.

'A bit.' He pulled a dissatisfied face. 'Uncle Bob came over and we went out for a posh tea at Wootton Castle.'

Ellie was just about to ask about Finn's dad when Finn blurted, 'By the way, Mrs Blix... I'm ... *we* are sorry that we didn't tell you about *us*. And that you had to find out the way you did. I hate secrets. People always get hurt.'

'I agree about that.'

'Hear, hear.' Sylvia passed mugs of steaming tea to everyone and sat down to eat her fish and chips.

'I hope you'll forgive us.' Finn's expression was sincere.

'It wasn't that we didn't care, Mum.' Zoe looked at Finn. 'Was it?'

He checked back with Zoe, as though seeking reassurance that he was going to say the right thing. 'We genuinely didn't know what to do for the best. We didn't want to upset you any more – after ... everything that's happened.'

'It always hurts when people don't tell you things, and I wish you had told me, but I can see why you didn't. What makes it hurt more is finding out at the same time as hearing that it was your mum that Dave had an affair with.'

'Sorry. We talked about it loads.' He shot a glance at Zoe. 'We knew about the affair but we felt that was his secret to tell you about.'

Ellie sighed. 'That's fair enough. It *was*.' She recalibrated. 'Like you, probably, I'm still reeling with shock about your mother, but at the same time, I'm Zoe's mum so...' She shifted her gaze onto Zoe. 'I want to make sure that *you* are OK.'

'Yeah, Mum. I told you. We're really happy.' She was holding onto Finn's arm, beaming up at him like a trusting child.

'How about you, Finn?' Ellie couldn't help thinking about Debbie saying that Andrea had been scared of him.

'To be honest, I have no idea how I feel about anything at the moment except Zoe.' He flashed a brief, courageous smile.

Ellie waited patiently.

'I'm really pleased Mum and I got the chance to spend a bit of time together. The last time we saw each other–' He broke off to blow his nose and to wipe tears from his face. 'We were screaming. It was horrible. I was so angry. I still am, in lots of ways.'

'That's understandable, considering what's happened.' Empathy ran through Sylvia's voice.

'Of course.' Ellie gathered her thoughts. Now was her chance to find out. 'Can I ask you about that?'

'Sure.'

'Your rows with your mum. None of them got physical or anything, did they?' She hoped he would understand her concern.

All eyes were on Finn.

His face clouded over. 'Physical? As in, me hitting her? Never.' His words were full of shock. 'I used to stomp about a lot and slam the door sometimes, but I've never laid a finger on Mum.' His attention was on Zoe. 'Is that what you're worried about? That I'm going to hit Zoe? Or are you secretly wondering if I killed my mum?'

Zoe put her hand on Finn's arm. '*Mumm.*' Her voice was disapproving.

'I have to ask. I'm sorry.'

Ellie could see Sylvia was itching to chip in and appreciated that she didn't.

'There was a phase where I was getting into fights with male friends. People at school. People I met. They were stupid scuffles. But I've never been violent with a woman – or any girlfriend.' He placed his hand on his chest. 'I give you my word. And I am angry with Mum. I've admitted it. But I *didn't* kill her.'

'It's true, Mum. Do you really think I'd be in a relationship with someone who hit me?'

Ellie was shaking her head. 'Not really, but to be honest, I'm still trying to make sense of all this new information. And sometimes people are so in love, they deny things or put up with them. I just don't want that for you, darling, that's all.'

It fitted with what she had picked up from Dave, with what others in the village had said.

'I've got a lot of things to sort out. I know that.' Finn kissed Zoe's forehead tenderly. 'But domestic violence isn't one of them, I promise you.' His gaze met Ellie's. 'Knowing that someone killed my mum though, wow, that's a whole other level.'

'Have the police put you in touch with Victim Support?'

'Yeah. Your husband is sorting it out. He suggested I do some counselling too. What's weird is that Mum and I were really close for years.' A softness, which Ellie hadn't seen before, spread over his face. 'We had lots of fun.' He chuckled as he seemed to be recalling fond memories. 'And suddenly…' His face clouded over, '…things changed.' This chimed with Debbie's comments.

'Do you know what it was?'

He was nodding. 'I started getting curious about my dad. I started asking lots of questions, and Mum wouldn't answer them.'

This wasn't news to Ellie, but she wanted to be sensitive and think carefully about what to say. 'This'll be something you can explore in counselling. I'm sure your mum was trying to protect you.' She paused. 'Will you be OK staying at your mother's place on your own? You're very welcome to come and stay with us at the windmill, if you'd like to. It can't be fun staying there with your mum gone. You can bring Mouse.'

'Thank you. I appreciate that. But I kind of feel a bit closer to mum being there. And Auntie Debbie and I are going to have to arrange her funeral.' He seemed to be clarifying his thoughts. 'It'd be nice to come over sometimes though. If that's alright?'

'Anytime.' Andrea's will came into Ellie's mind. 'Speaking of her wishes, did your mum leave a will? Debbie wasn't sure.'

'Oh, yes. That I do know about. I don't know the details, but she told me she'd been to update it.'

So, Julia was right.

'You've said you don't know the details, but did she give you any hint who her beneficiaries are? It could be extremely relevant.'

Finn was shaking his head. 'I'll hunt for it tomorrow. Given she'd just revised it, it must be in her belongings or with the solicitor. I'll let you know.'

'Great. Thanks. I'm afraid this question's a bit delicate so...'

'Go on.'

'Are you taking any drugs?' Ellie checked Zoe's reaction.

Sylvia sucked in a breath.

'Nope.' Finn was shaking his head. 'I was taking loads when Mum kicked me out. But I've been clean for over two years now.' He squeezed Zoe's hand.

'Well done.'

Finn's face lit up. 'Thank you. Your daughter refuses to go out with anyone who takes drugs, so I've got a pretty good incentive.' He smiled and it transformed his face. The pain receded and genuine happiness shone through. 'I need to know what happened to Mum though and who killed her. That's why I'm pleased you and Sylvia and Zoe are looking into it. I know you and Mum fell out, and she ... um ... told me why. But I also know that you go back a long way. And she said she *trusted* you.'

Ellie gasped. 'Oh. I ... er ... didn't know that.'

'Mum was dying. It wasn't weeks. But she had developed headaches, problems with her vision, flashing lights and mood swings. And the occasional blackout.' He stopped and drew breath. 'I didn't know any of this until two days ago, when I got back to Mum's, so I'm still taking it in myself. The tumour had started to creep into parts of her brain that controlled her inhibitions. It meant she could behave erratically.'

'I'm so sorry.'

'This is the thing. Because she knew she was going to die, she had started ticking things off her bucket list. She had just been given a big part in the spring play and she was really excited about it.'

'Yes. I heard about that. I'm glad. The other thing I wanted to ask you about is your dad.' Ellie paused, allowing Finn to prepare a bit. She had heard Debbie's account and wanted to hear things from Finn's perspective. 'What's the situation with him? Have you heard from him?'

Finn froze for a few moments, then shook his head.

Ellie saw the anguish on his face.

'Mum said she had been in touch with him recently, but we didn't get the opportunity to talk about him, so I don't know what they discussed or what his views are. As far as I know, he's always refused to have anything to do with me, so I'm not holding out much hope that things will change.'

'Do you know who he is?' Ellie held her breath. Poor Finn. He'd been through so much.

Zoe stroked his arm.

'No. Her view was that, because he didn't want to know me, it was better for me not to know.' He pursed his lips and his eyes narrowed. 'She had recently changed her mind and was going to tell me though.'

'I can appreciate that you would have liked to have had the choice of getting in touch, but she probably thought she was protecting you.' Someone was going to have to tell him – and quickly. She would speak to Debbie.

'Yes. And then she was killed.'

Ellie felt Finn's pain. It seemed so cruel for him to be on the verge of getting answers, only for them to be snatched away from him for good. Rejection was etched on his face and in his eyes.

Ellie scrolled through the list of questions on her phone to check she was covering the most important things. 'The night your mum died I went over to her house. Was it you who had been reading her email?'

'Yes. I knew the CID presence meant she'd been killed, and I wanted to see what I could find in her email. I had her password as I'd needed to use her computer.'

'Were you there when I arrived? Was it you who left on a motorbike?'

'No. I was out.' Finn frowned. 'I went to meet Zoe. And I don't have a bike.'

Chapter 21

DAY 3 – 23rd Dec, 7am

After the conveyor belt of revelations the day before, Ellie didn't sleep well. Her dreams were a swirling mixture of scenes from *The Canterbury Murders*, and interactions with Dave, Andrea, Finn, Debbie and Sue. In her fevered imagination, everyone in the village had acquired a motorbike, and they were all leaving poisoned cake on each other's doorsteps. She woke with a heavy feeling. Had she taken on too much, deciding, on top of everything else, to help find Andrea's killer? It was a relief to have Sylvia and Zoe's help – and now Finn's too.

She'd only just tumbled out of bed and started cleaning her teeth when her phone rang. The number had been withheld.

'Blix Blitz,' she said, trying not to spit toothpaste over her phone.

It was Sue. She was in a panic, gabbling down the line. 'The police want to talk to me about Andrea's death.'

Ellie was taken back to the fish and chip shop, with Gemma telling Roxie that Sue had called Andrea a selfish woman and a bad mother. 'It'll be routine. They'll be talking to everyone who had a disagreement with Andrea.' She forced a laugh. 'Like I said at the hall – that includes me.'

'But I don't...' Sue was stammering, '...know what to tell them.' She was clearly anxious about the interview.

Ellie spat the toothpaste out and tried to be reassuring. 'Just answer their questions. Tell the truth.'

Rebus was settled on the floor in the doorway, watching her. Downstairs she could hear music. Sylvia and Zoe chatting.

'That's easy for you to say. You've been a detective's wife for years.' She started muttering away under her breath.

Ellie swilled her mouth out and wiped her lips. There was something Sue wasn't saying. 'Whatever they ask, just answer honestly.'

'Would you come to the police station with me? I... I don't want to go on my own.' She wanted to go as soon as Ellie could make it.

Ellie had enough on her plate with Zoe off sick, and she was keen to avoid the station as the police wanted to speak to her too. Plus, she didn't know Sue well. 'I've got a couple of jobs near Deal this morning. If it'll make you feel more confident about going, how about I pick you up from the bistro after those, say 10am? I can come with you.' Ellie could give Rebus a quick run on the green first.

'Thank you. Ten's fine.' Sue paused, and Ellie got the feeling she hadn't finished. 'You will come, won't you? I must...'

'Course.'

'It's just...' She stopped and then whispered, '*I'm really scared, Ellie.*'

'Don't worry.' Ellie was mentally running through her day. 'Stay at home if you're scared. Give me a couple of hours to get my jobs done and I'll be there, I promise.' She rang off. Her stomach sank. She just hoped she could take Sue to the police station without bumping into Dave again.

She grabbed her towel and opened the shower door. Sue's tone was still in her ears. Her urgency. Her panic. In her haste to get on with her day, Ellie realised she had been a bit brusque. She should at least have asked her what she was scared about.

Chapter 22

7.15am

Ellie had just got out of the shower when her phone started ringing again. It was Laura, one of her regular cleaners.

'Morning. Really sorry, I'm not going to be able to do my jobs until this afternoon.'

Ellie's heart sank. She was exhausted.

'Aidan has had a temperature all night and it's up further this morning.'

'Oh no, sorry to hear that.' She knew how terrifying it was. Simon had been prone to fevers as a child.

'His dad is at his parents' 'til Christmas Eve. I'm just off to the GP's. If I can get someone to have him, I'll do my jobs later.'

'No problem. I'll cover them. Let me know how he is.'

The two women chatted for a few moments and rang off.

Ellie got up, let Rebus out and made coffee. She sat down at the kitchen table with her work diary and eyed first Laura's jobs for the day and then hers. There was no way Ellie could absorb Laura's day into her own.

Fifteen minutes later, she'd sent requests for a supply cleaner to all the agencies. She got dressed, and by the time she returned to her laptop, notifications were pinging into her inbox, one by one, saying they had no free staff.

Ellie's neck and shoulders felt tense. She hated being down to the wire like this when things went wrong. Having no safety net, no backup. Her aching back was standard these days, and her neck and shoulders were still sore from yesterday's job in a large family home where the owner *insisted* that she moved all the furniture before she hoovered. She would either have to cancel Laura's jobs or get some help.

She ran her eye over Laura's day again. She had three regulars, starting with Martha's house at 8am. Then the local school at 2pm, and after that, the travel agents in Dover. The last one was a large office premises, but it was light cleaning and amongst her biggest payers. With large winter bills on the windmill, and without Dave's salary to help, she couldn't afford to lose customers.

Sally was right. In the new year, she'd restructure things, take on some more staff. But right now – who could she ask to help her? Her first thought was Finn. He was young and strong. As far as she'd gleaned, he was just starting as a gardener and wasn't working much. He might fancy a bit of distraction and some extra money.

She dialled his number.

He picked up straightaway. 'Wow, this is early, Mrs B.'

'Morning. Sorry.' She filled him in about Laura and the jobs. 'Could you help me out?'

'Martha?'

'Yes. Her place is first. That OK?'

'Nope.' His voice was more strident. 'No way am I doing that woman's cleaning. Sorry.'

'OK.' She couldn't press him. He sounded adamant. Something must've happened with his mother. She'd have to leave that for now.

'I can do the school though.'

'You're sure?'

'Yep.'

'Great. It's at 2pm. I'll text you the address and meet you there to explain what we do. See you later.' She rang off. The only other person she could think of, who wasn't going to be at work, was Sally.

She dialled Sally's number.

'Hey-heyy.' Sally's voice was echoey. Ellie heard whispering in the background. 'I'm just about to get in the shower.' She giggled.

'I get the feeling I'm disturbing something, so I'll just say what I rang for.' She told Sally about Laura and Finn. 'So, it's just a light clean at Martha's at 8am. Happy to pay. I've drawn a blank with all the agencies. Christmas, I guess.'

Sally agreed, said she'd meet Ellie at the Old Post Office in an hour, then rang off.

Phew. Everything was sorted.

She texted Laura, letting her know not to worry about work today and wishing Aidan a speedy recovery.

A few minutes later, Ellie was ready to leave. She sent Rebus off to his bed and opened the front door of the windmill.

A woman was holding up a press badge on a lanyard. She was mid-thirties and had a tight smile on shiny lips. She had cherry-red hair in a top knot and was wearing a long, quilted coat. 'Morning. *The Wootton Gazette.*'

Ellie groaned inwardly. Katie Douglas was the last person she wanted to see. They'd had several spats over the years when Katie wrote bitchy articles about local people, most recently when she'd compiled a hatchet job on Ellie's cleaning company.

'I'd like to ask you a few questions about the death of Andrea Burdett. A source has told me that you were at her house the evening she died.'

Ellie closed the front door of the windmill behind her. 'What source?'

'I can't divulge that, I'm afraid. Are you denying you were at her house then?'

'I'm not going to comment. I need to get to my first job. You remember my *cleaning company,* don't you? The one with…' Ellie made air quotes, '"…lazy staff who run their feet over the carpets instead of hoovering and who rifle through customer's fridges"?' She zapped the jeep's locks with the remote.

Katie flickered a cold, tight smile and continued. 'I'm writing a piece on Mrs Burdett's background. I understand you both went to the same school and had a falling out?'

'That was a long time ago and it's public knowledge around here. I doubt local readers will find it remotely interesting.'

'Except when someone dies, the police are always interested in the victim's enemies. Anyone with a grudge.'

'We weren't *enemies*. We just fell out in sixth form and haven't been friends since.'

'Have the police interviewed you about the murder?'

'No, they haven't.'

'You've got to be expecting a knock at the door, surely? Especially after the row the two of you had last week when she came round to your house. Or do you get, you know, *special treatment,'* she pulled an annoying face, 'with your ex on the force?'

'Don't be ridiculous.'

Katie shrugged and her top-knot bobbed from side to side. 'Harry's asked me to get a quote from you on why you went over to Andrea's house.'

'I've no idea who Harry is, and I've given this information to the police.'

Katie gave an exaggerated eye roll. 'Suit yourself. Of course, we know about your husband's affair with Mrs Burdett, so we can always write about that. That must've hurt. On top of your *feud*?'

Blimey. What a cow.

Katie had always managed to wheedle things out of people. It made her a formidable reporter and enemy.

Ellie swallowed hard and stowed her bag in the jeep. 'That's none of your business.'

'Except it might have given you further reason to feel aggrieved towards her?'

Ellie stopped what she was doing. 'What are you suggesting exactly?'

'Nothing. Just asking.'

'You mean like you *asked* a disgruntled ex-employee of mine to tell a load of lies about me and my company that time?'

'What can I tell you? Just doing my job. It was a very popular article. But I'd like to think we could move on from that.'

The cheek of her.

Suddenly, a thought occurred to Ellie. What if she could somehow turn the interaction round and get some information out of Katie? The woman seemed to know how to extract information out of everyone. She might have found out more about the poisoned cake. It was worth a go, surely? She would have to summon all her acting skills. 'Actually, you're right,' Ellie lied. 'The most important thing for the community is finding Andrea's killer.' She gestured for Katie to come closer and dropped her voice to a confidential whisper. 'Thank goodness the police can carry out stomach and urine analysis.' She was trying to imply that she knew what food had contained the thallium, in the hope Katie would confirm it. 'The thing with thallium is that it's slow-acting, odourless and tasteless.' She didn't say that Zoe had researched it on the internet.

'Exactly.' Katie lowered her voice too. 'You probably know this from your ex. Harry's a whizz on this stuff because he knows someone at the lab. Andrea's stomach didn't contain thallium. It was in her urine.'

Of course.

Zoe's research. Ellie had absorbed the information but not really thought about what it meant in practice. 'Yes,' she nodded, encouragingly. 'Because thallium's slow-acting, Andrea must've ingested the poison a couple of days earlier, and it wouldn't have been in her stomach or her blood.' She was still bluffing. Dave was going to be furious with her. 'So, they had to test her urine.' Did that mean the poison had or hadn't been in the cake?

'That's what our source at the lab said. Thankfully, the police tested all the food and drink in her house.'

'They're always thorough.'

Come on, Katie. Spit it out. What was the poison in?

'Luckily, they checked her bedroom for samples, and found the dregs of a cup of tea that she'd not quite finished and had left by her bed. Had thallium in it. Bingo.'

Bingo indeed. Ellie could hardly contain herself. Somehow, the information she'd overheard was wrong, but that didn't matter now. 'I couldn't believe it when I found out that *that* was what the thallium was in.'

This time she wasn't lying.

Ellie bundled the last of her cleaning kit into the jeep, jumped in, said goodbye and zoomed off. It had been a strange encounter, but then it always was with Katie, and Ellie had got some vital information out of her. She just wished she could get away from the feeling that she was going to pay for it.

Chapter 23

8am

The first thing Ellie did when she arrived at Martha's was text Zoe and tell her about the tea. She asked her to find out what Finn knew about someone making Andrea a cup of tea, which she'd either taken to her bedroom herself or which she was brought.

At 8am on the dot, Ellie and Sally were on the doorstep of Martha's beautiful home. The Old Post Office was originally three cottages that had been knocked through. To their right, the River Wootton gleamed in the morning light.

Ellie told Sally about her conversation with Katie, the reporter. 'I've made a massive mistake about the thallium.' She repeated what she had learnt from Katie.

'How did you manage that?'

No-one answered, so Ellie used the company keys to let Sally and herself in. There was no Oscar at the door. Perhaps Martha had taken him out for a walk. 'I heard Dave repeat back "cake" when he asked about her stomach contents and assumed this meant that's what the poison was in.'

'Did you hear the whole conversation?'

'That's the thing. I only heard Dave's side.'

'Oh Ells. You doughnut. The person might have said something like, "the thallium was in a cup of tea, but she had a load of cake in her stomach too", and Dave could have simply repeated back, "yeah ... thallium ... cake".'

'I know,' Ellie whispered. 'It was a stupid assumption. Katie actually did me a huge favour.' She raised her voice. 'Martha?' Double-checking was customary before they ploughed into a customer's house. 'It's Blix Blitz.' She was relieved Martha was out. It made jobs so much easier and quicker when cleaners didn't have to make polite conversation with customers and contend with their surveillance.

The two of them carried their equipment and vacuum cleaners into the spacious hall. Ellie knew the layout, as she'd cleaned Martha's house a couple of times before. Martha had preserved many of the Post Office's original features: the postal slats, a franking bench, the old post room. Ellie and Sally quickly split up and started on different rooms, Sally downstairs, Ellie up.

Martha's bathroom was clean, bright and white with floor to ceiling tiles on two walls. There were no children's toys round the bath, no wet towels and clothes on the floor.

Ellie cleaned the bath, basin, toilet, floor and mirrors. While she worked, she racked her brain for how she could find out who had put thallium in Andrea's tea.

Next door, the spare bedroom was clutter-free. No piles of laundry on the bed, no boxes or junk. Ellie dusted and hoovered the landing and was soon in Martha's bedroom. This was always the room that felt the most personal to Ellie when she was cleaning people's houses. It was where her clients dreamt their dreams, where they lay awake worrying about whatever was bothering them. It was where they explored the innermost crevices of their minds.

Over the years, she'd developed the habit of seeing her clients in purely professional terms, even when she knew them personally. They were customers. She was just providing a service. That meant she didn't gawp at their family photos, their kids' drawings on the fridge, their laundry. And she didn't allow herself to think too much about any of their property. But today – perhaps because she was tired and her defences were down – she found herself thinking about the woman whose house they were in.

Andrea's best friend.

Martha had lived in Lower Wootton for – what? Fifteen years? Something like that. What had Debbie said?

They'd known each other for years.

That Martha had moved to Lower Wootton when her son died.

Ellie scoped the room. There weren't any photos. She cast her mind back to when she'd cleaned for Martha before. Had she seen any family snaps downstairs? Given her son had died, wouldn't she have had pictures out to remember his life?

Ellie wondered briefly how she'd feel if Zoe had died. Even thinking about it created a tight ball in her stomach. She imagined surrounding herself with as many of her daughter's things as she could.

But – everyone was different, and perhaps Martha had found this was the best way of coming to terms with her son's death.

'Ells.' Sally's voice came up the stairs. 'You got hoover bags?'

'Hang on. They're in the jeep.' She placed the vacuum hose on the floor. 'Coming now.' Downstairs, she found Sally in the lounge.

'It's a gorgeous place, isn't it? I haven't been here before.' Sally surveyed the room as though she was assessing it for purchase.

Ellie followed Sally's gaze. And probably because she'd just been thinking about it, she found her eyes hunting for photos. She approached the mantelpiece.

Clock.

Cream candles.

Warm white fairy lights.

Christmassy pine cones.

She scanned the walls and sideboard. 'Is it me, or is it weird that she doesn't have any photos? There aren't any upstairs either. Not even in her bedroom.'

'Oh... I hadn't...' Sally performed a similar check to the one Ellie had just made. 'Actually – you're right.' She chuckled. 'Mind you – you have got *loads* at your place.'

'True. Each to their own, I guess. Don't know why I'm thinking about it really.' Ellie jangled her car keys. 'I'll get that hoover bag.' She checked the clock on the mantelpiece. 'We should be done in about fifteen minutes.'

Ellie was back from the jeep in a few moments, and while she was downstairs, she moved the furniture for Sally so her friend could easily hoover. The two of them nattered away.

Sally had done the kitchen and dining room, so, once they'd finished the lounge, she followed Ellie upstairs and into Martha's bedroom. 'It's just the sort of house I'd expect her to live in. Old, beautifully renovated, clean and tidy.'

'And *no clutter*.'

They both laughed.

It was a huge room. The bed – a super king-size deluxe – nestled in one part, bang in the centre of the wall, facing two sets of floor-to-ceiling French windows. White walls, white bed linen and full-length, white voile curtains.

'Peaceful, isn't it?' Sally seemed to be taking in the ambience. 'Gosh. Check this out. She's got a walk-in wardrobe.' She pulled the doors open, and suddenly a wooden box and a lamp came crashing down from a wall of shelves. The light rolled over and the box spilled open on the carpet.

Ellie rushed over. Fortunately, the lamp was unbroken.

'Oh gawd,' Sally said apologetically. 'Where was that hiding?' Her eyes fell to the floor, where stacks of photos spread over the carpet. '*This* is how she keeps it tidy up here.'

Through the doorway, metal shelving racks lined both sides of the small room. Each one was piled high with boxes. A rail hung along the wall ahead, carrying clothes on hangers. Dresses, coats, blouses, all colour coordinated.

'Look at this.' Sally pointed at the photos. 'These are the family snaps you were talking about.'

A strange feeling crept over Ellie and she was overcome with sadness for Martha. 'C'mon. We need to pack them back up.' She kneeled down to help Sally, and her eyes fell on a photograph.

Ellie and Sally stared at the image in front of them.

It was Martha's baby, lying on his back on a mat. Martha and a man were leaning over, smiling at the baby's pudgy limbs, fine blond hair and porcelain cheeks. Ellie picked the image up and turned it over. The date was written in faded ink pen alongside: *Nate*.

'What a lovely name. Presumably, the man is the father.' Ellie's voice was a whisper. She laid the photo back down.

Next to it was a later image, a mousey-haired toddler-Nate in shorts and sandals. And an older Nate, a perky little boy in school uniform, unruly light brown hair, cheeks flushed with excitement.

'How awful to lose your child.' She stared at one picture, then another.

There was Martha and Nate with friends and with other children, but apart from that one image of a man when Nate was a new-born baby, his father didn't seem to appear in later pictures.

Sally had her hand over her mouth. 'I feel dreadful,' she whispered. 'I knew she'd come to live here after her son died, but I hadn't stopped to think about the reality of that situation. Or what that might be like for her. To think about ... *all this.*' She gestured to the array of images.

Martha's secret life.

'I know they divorced, but I wonder what happened with the father?' Sally seemed to be thinking. 'I don't recall ever seeing Martha with a partner, do you?'

Ellie shook her head. Suddenly, one image caught her eye and she gasped. It showed the same newborn Nate as she'd seen previously. Blond hair and alabaster skin, in Martha's arms. They sat opposite a young Andrea who was beaming at beautiful baby Finn on her lap. He was waving his arms around.

Ellie's fingers reached for the image. She picked it up and scrutinised it. The two women were sitting at a garden table in summer sunshine. Both were smiling and laughing, not a care in the world. Both had their beautiful babies on their laps.

Sally leaned over to get a closer look. 'Wow. Their children knew each other too.' She stared at Ellie. 'I had no idea.'

'I didn't either.' Ellie was shaking her head, uncomfortable at what they were seeing. 'C'mon. We need to put these away. It's not right. They're private.' She took a last quick look at Andrea and Martha and began hurriedly stacking the photos and putting them back.

Sally followed suit and they quickly repacked the box, stowed it back on the shelf and closed the closet doors.

A few minutes later, Ellie had just opened Martha's front door to leave when her mobile rang. She put the vacuum cleaner down on the ground, leaving the door open. 'Blix Blitz Cleaning Services.'

It was a withheld number, a lady wanting to book some cleaning dates for her elderly father for the new year. 'Can I take your number, and I'll give you a call back once I'm back in the car with my diary? I'll only be a couple of minutes.'

She searched Martha's brightly lit hall for a notepad. 'Hold on a sec. I need something to write on.'

By the lamp, there was a jotter. She grabbed it up and was about to start writing when she noticed the imprint from writing on the previous page. In capital letters, Martha had written 'GRAHAM'S VIDEO'. Ellie jotted down the woman's number on top of it and rang off. She tore the slip of paper off the pad and tucked it in her pocket.

As she and Sally carried the cleaning equipment out to the car, Ellie was still pondering the photographs they'd seen. Did they mean anything, and why were they hidden away?

Chapter 24

9.45am

Ellie left Martha's house with her mind on fire. She couldn't stop thinking about the image of Martha and Andrea with their two babies.

She reached Sue's bistro, the Wootton Wine Bar, fifteen minutes early and parked outside. The timber shop door was closed. White fairy lights hung in rows across the inside of the shop front, glowing in the December morning light. They didn't open until midday.

Ellie pushed the main door, hoping one of the staff might be setting up, but it was locked. She peered through the window. Not a soul around. She remembered the bistro had a rear garden and gate opening into a lane – she and Dave had been there a few times – so she nipped around the back. But when she got there, the gate was locked from the inside and Sue had left her yellow golfing umbrella leaning up against the fence. Ellie took out her phone and dialled Sue's number.

Voicemail. Ellie left a message.

Perhaps she'd decided to go to the police on her own? Ellie scrolled through her texts. Nothing from Sue. No missed calls from her. That was strange. Where was she? Ellie remembered the tone in her voice on the phone earlier.

Ellie got back in the jeep. She pulled her diary out of her bag. She had the school and the travel agent. Hopefully, she could take Sue to the police station sometime later, if that was what she wanted still. She pinged her a text and opened Facebook.

The first item in her feed was on *the Wootton Gazette's* page. It had a picture of Ellie and Andrea arguing outside the windmill. Ellie looked up from her phone screen, half expecting to see Dave glowering at her over the steering wheel because the article carried the headline: DOES LOCAL CLEANER KNOW MORE THAN SHE'S SAYING?

Damn woman. She might have known Katie would write something like that. It was now even more pressing for her to find out who had killed Andrea and put an end to all this speculation in the village. She googled the number of the paper on her phone and the surname of the editor Katie had mentioned. She dialled. 'Morning. Harry Stow, please. I want to make a complaint about an article and headline.'

Chapter 25

10am

On her way out of the village, Ellie stopped at the hair salon on the high street. It was a pretty premises with large windows. Inside, carols were playing from tiny Bluetooth speakers, and the room smelled of chocolate and spice.

'I'm glad I'm not the only one who makes themselves look ridiculous at Christmas,' Ellie joked with Trisha, the receptionist, who had felt reindeer horns on her head and was tucking into a piece of chocolate log.

Trisha laughed, put the last piece of cake into her mouth and tapped at her keyboard.

'Listen, I've got a spare fifteen minutes and I thought I'd check to see if I could get a fringe trim?' Ellie let her ponytail out and flattened her fringe to show how long it had grown. 'I can hardly see what I'm doing. I nearly took the dog scissors to it last week.'

The two women laughed.

Trisha checked the clock. 'If you're OK with her doing it dry, Helen can do it now for you. She's just finished, and her next client is running late.'

'I can spray it and cut it,' came Helen's voice from the back. She was the salon's owner. 'It'll be fine. Have a seat, Ellie, love. I'll be out in a sec. Just checking to see what my Roxie has put on Facebook. She and Gemma are as wild as anything at the moment. Get Ellie a coffee, Trisha, will you, please?'

Ellie laughed as she remembered hearing the two girls in the fish and chip shop, clearly the worse for wear. 'Will do. Thanks.'

She was walking over to the seat next to the window when Helen called out again from the back room, 'Oh my word. Ellie, have you seen the article about you in the Wootton Gazette? It's on their Facebook page and already has seventy-eight comments.'

Ellie groaned. 'I saw it earlier. I've asked the editor to take it down but he won't. Says it's "cutting-edge investigative journalism".'

'I'd call it gossip and speculation,' Helen chimed in. 'And it's stirring up trouble for you too. That Katie

Douglas wrote an awful piece about this place. I think it was in the same series as the one she did on Blix Blitz.'

'The sooner Andrea's murder is solved, the better. All this suspicion isn't good for anyone's health.'

A woman's back was facing Ellie in a black gown, a full head of foils, head tilted forwards and reading a magazine. In the mirror, Ellie saw who it was. 'Jane. How are you? Saw your gorgeous set the other day. Any decisions on the panto?'

Jane put her magazine down. 'Hey. Sorry to hear about this local paper business.' She gave Ellie a sympathetic smile. 'Yes, after much deliberation, we've decided to go ahead with the performances as planned.' She was grinning. 'The first night will now be the dress rehearsal as we've lost a day.'

'That's great news. I'm so pleased. I bet the cast are too.'

She beamed at Ellie. 'Thanks so much for posting in the village Facebook group. We've had quite a few people offer assistance.'

'It was nothing. Pleased to help.'

'Zoe's obviously still not well, but she's encouraged Finn to join us. He's got some free time, I gather, while he's building up his gardening business.'

'I saw his business cards. Going to be super handy for us. The back garden at the windmill is like a rewilding experiment.'

'Coffee or tea, ladies?' Trisha shouted over at them.

Jane and Ellie conveyed their preferences.

Ellie remembered she'd wanted to ask Jane about Andrea. Grabbing the opportunity, she checked to see where Trisha was and lowered her voice.

'Jane? I'm trying to help find out what happened to Andrea. Mike told me you overheard her telling someone to leave her alone. Did you get any sense of whether she was talking to a stranger or someone she knew?'

Jane paused to think. 'She said, "I've told you before", so she must've known the person and already asked them to leave her alone.'

'Yes, I thought that.' Ellie was grateful for the corroboration. 'Anything else that might be important?'

'Yes. The "you've ruined my life" comment implied that what the person had been doing was serious.' Jane's face was pensive. 'She also said, "I've told you. He doesn't want to".'

'Ah. That's interesting. Mike didn't tell me that last bit. I wonder who "he" was? Thank you. Quite apart from my fringe trim, I'm pleased I popped in.'

Ellie checked to see where Trisha was. 'One last thing. Has anyone complained about the casting of Andrea as lead for the spring play?'

'Just Sue.' Jane rolled her eyes. 'But that's par for the course. She complained about Andrea getting a tiny part in the panto, too.'

'Did you get a sense of what her problem was with Andrea? Did she not like her?'

'I don't think it was that. More that Sue's a perfectionist. And she got irritated that Andrea missed rehearsals and forgot her lines.'

Ellie was about to defend Andrea.

'When she told us she was ill, it made sense, but I don't think Sue knew about it at the time. She simply thought Andrea was being flaky.'

'Here we are, ladies.' Trisha's voice was the cue to change the subject. She handed Ellie and Jane their drinks and a slice of chocolate log each.

'Ooh, lovely. Thank you,' Ellie laughed. 'I'll come here again.'

While she waited for Helen, she wondered who could have ruined Andrea's life. Had she been talking to her stalker? Or could she have been talking to Finn's father? And how did Sue fit into it all?

Chapter 26

10am

Sylvia agreed to go with Zoe and Finn to Andrea's house so Finn could find his mother's will. It was freezing when they arrived. Mouse was at the door to meet them. Finn quickly made a fire in the open plan kitchen-diner, and Sylvia settled herself into one of the armchairs by the fireplace with Mouse on her lap. Sylvia adored open fires. She watched as the beautiful ash logs caught light. They crackled and spat, and she felt the heat warming her bones. She was a few rows into a new knitting project. On the drinks table beside her, she had a ball of wool. If Andrea hadn't been tragically killed, everything would have been perfect.

Up the other end of the room, Finn and Zoe were playing Christmas songs through one of their phones. They were pulling out drawers, hunting through Andrea's belongings. The floor was like an obstacle course, littered with piles of photographs, documents and bills.

Sylvia chuckled as Zoe and Finn found a way to work together. Zoe wanted to do things systematically; Finn's approach was more haphazard, and every now and then they'd clash and negotiate a way forward. Ellie was right to be concerned about Finn's anger. Any mother would feel that way about her daughter's boyfriend. But Finn deserved a chance, and Sylvia liked how he was with Zoe. She was headstrong and passionate, like her mother, and Finn was gentle with her.

Suddenly, Zoe gasped. 'Look at these.' In one hand, she had an envelope, in the other she had a piece of paper. She was kneeling on the rug next to a plastic wallet file. 'Brian Silk has been writing to your mum.'

'What?' Sylvia sat bolt upright in her chair, nearly dropping her knitting. 'After a stalking offence, he's likely to be on probation. I'd bet money on there being terms to it, like not being allowed to contact Andrea or come within a specified distance.'

'Well, this is evidence that he *has* been contacting her.' She held up a bunch of envelopes. 'All from him.'

She read aloud. 'It will not do. My feelings will not be repressed. You must allow me to tell you how ardently I admire and love you.' She stared at Finn, then her gran. 'He's quoting from Jane flipping Austen.'

'What else does he say?' Sylvia had put her knitting down and could hardly contain herself.

Zoe skimmed the letter. 'You're the woman for me... We are destined to be together... You're my reason for living... I've changed... you've misunderstood my intentions... I just want to talk ... to explain ... can we meet? I know where you live... I'm going to come round–'

'What an absolute creep. Let me see.' Finn leaped to her side.

Zoe passed him the letter and opened another one.

'He says he's not far away.' He muttered under his breath.

'In this one, he says he likes the wisteria up the back of the house.' Zoe clamped her hand over her mouth.

'He's been here, then.'

'Unless he checked the house out on Google's Street View?' Zoe retrieved her phone from her back pocket and started tapping at the screen.

Finn carried on skimming the letters.

'Nope.' She held out her phone for Finn to see. 'You can't see the wisteria on Street View. It's round the back and obscured by a tree.'

'He must've been here. Why didn't Mum tell me this pondlife was writing to her?'

Zoe placed her hand on his shoulder.

Sylvia spoke. 'You'd only just got back in touch. Maybe she didn't want to burden you?' She selected her words carefully, remembering what Debbie had told her and Ellie about Finn not knowing who his dad was. 'Perhaps there were a few things she wanted to talk to you about and she was choosing her time?'

Finn wheeled round.

Zoe was frowning. 'Surely Silk couldn't have poisoned Andrea? She would hardly have invited him in for a cup of tea.'

'Very unlikely,' Sylvia said.

'He must know she's dead,' said Zoe. 'It's all over the news.'

'We'll have to tell the police about these letters and that Silk has been here,' Sylvia stated. 'In case they don't know.' She shivered at the thought of poor Andrea, scared that the vile man was going to turn up. Had she been here when he had?

'The letters were right at the back of the cupboard under her cookbooks. The cops might not have seen them.' Zoe spun round and surveyed the room. 'I'm going to keep searching,' she said to Finn. 'See if I can find her will. Is it OK to check in her bedroom, babe?'

'Sure.'

Sylvia shuffled over to the sink. Her mind was in a whirl. She filled the kettle and switched it on to boil. She had left a message for her probation officer friend, from her time working at Social Services, but hadn't heard back from him. She knew what workloads were like. She would try him again if she could think of anything he would be allowed to tell her.

She got cups and tea bags from the cabinet and waited for the kettle to boil. Silk's letters had stirred her up. But there was something else on her mind, and that was, who was going to tell Finn who his dad was – and when? Part of her hoped he and Zoe might find something that mentioned him, so that he would at least now know.

A few moments later, Zoe came charging in. 'I've found them. I've found your mum's wills.' She shot over to Finn. 'At least I'm pretty sure this is the new one. It's got a red seal on the back.' She handed him a white envelope. 'This is the old one which she's opened – or someone has.'

'Where were they?' He slid his finger under the seal.

'She had a shoe box in one of her wardrobes.'

Finn opened the sealed document and scanned it. 'Dated a month ago. Estate beneficiaries ... Debbie and me. The executor is Uncle Bob.'

'This is her old one.' Zoe's face was full of anxiety. She passed the document to Finn.

'This one's dated two years ago.' He looked up. 'That would have been after she kicked me out.' He carried on reading. 'Here we go. In this one, her sole beneficiary was Debbie. Bob as executor.'

Sylvia took the milk from the fridge. 'That's quite a change.' She was collecting her thoughts. 'Are you absolutely sure Debbie was here when your mum said she had changed her will?'

Debbie had said she and her husband were hard up.

'Yes.' He pointed at the kitchen table. 'It was only a couple of days ago. We were all sitting there. Mum, Debbie, Uncle Bob and me. I'm gonna get her over here now. I want to know why she lied.'

'Hold on. I'm going to ring Mum.' Zoe's cheeks drained of colour as she faced her boyfriend. 'I'm really sorry, but this gives your aunt a motive to kill your mother.' She swiped her phone and dialled. 'Hey, Mum. Can you talk?'

'Yep, I'm on hands free. What's up?'

'Are you in the village?'

'Just leaving. Why?'

'We've got two massive developments. Can you come to Andrea's?'

'I'm on my way to a customer but I can turn round. Give me about ten minutes, OK?'

Sylvia got out another mug. She had the feeling things were all about to unravel.

Chapter 27

10.45am

When Ellie got out of the jeep at Andrea's house, Zoe was waiting for her. She was biting her nails.

'You OK, lovey? What's happened?'

Zoe blurted out what they'd learnt about Brian Silk.

Ellie mulled over the implications. 'Those letters are further evidence he's in the area. You've told your dad, haven't you?'

'Yes.'

They walked up the path to the house.

Sylvia was standing in the doorway. She had a phone stuck to her ear. 'Only physically dangerous with people he's obsessed with. Right.' She repeated back what she'd heard. 'And people who thwart him. Got it. Thanks, Ralph. No, I appreciate you can't tell me any more. You've been very helpful.' She rang off. 'That was Silk's probation officer. We've known each other for years. He's confirmed what I suspected. Silk *did* have conditions to his probation, and he has broken them.'

'Well done,' Ellie said to Sylvia. 'That's fine. We don't need to know what the conditions are. The police can deal with that. Just knowing he's broken them is enough. Combined with the letters, hopefully, it will get him sent back inside when they catch him.'

'You heard what Ralph said about Silk's risk levels?'

'Yeah. I don't like the sound of "thwart".'

'Nor do I. It means anyone who stops him from doing what he wants to. And Ralph thinks he's in the area too.'

'Ugh. As if Andrea's death isn't enough to worry about. Now we've got a stalker on the loose.' Ellie put her arm round Zoe's waist. 'Let's go in. I'm freezing, and you need to keep warm.'

'We've got the fire on,' Sylvia said.

'You said two developments?' Ellie reminded Zoe.

Zoe told her mum about the will revision.

'Oh wow. That's a big change then. Any thoughts, Sylvia? You're the family systems expert.'

'It confirms what Finn told us. His mum wanted to put the past behind them and make sure her son was OK.'

'Yes. What I don't understand though is why Debbie said she didn't know whether Andrea had a will.'

'We're about to find out.' Her tone was grave. 'Finn has just rung her and she's on her way. She was at the vicarage. Think she's discussing funeral arrangements.'

*

When Debbie arrived twenty minutes later, Finn was inside with Zoe, trying to calm down. He was annoyed that Debbie was having discussions about Andrea's funeral without him.

Ellie went out to meet them and was surprised to see she had brought her husband. They weren't on their shiny BMW motorbikes. They were in an old, lime-green Nissan Micra which had a dent in the rear. If Ellie hadn't known better, she would have thought they'd borrowed the run-around of a university student son or daughter.

Debbie smiled when she saw Ellie but there was no warmth in her eyes, just a jitteriness to her overall manner. 'This is Ben,' she said simply.

Ben wasn't at all what Ellie had imagined. He was much shorter than his wife and looked at least ten years older. He had a slight build, pale skin and wore metal-framed glasses which pinched the muscle at his temples. Ellie couldn't help noticing that he walked behind his wife, with his head slightly downcast. There was definitely a story here and she had a feeling it was about to come out.

They were soon in Andrea's open plan kitchen. Sylvia was busy making tea – one of her favourite roles. Ellie showed them to the big oak table and gestured to Finn, who was lurking by the fire, to join them.

'Alright,' Finn said curtly. 'Have you arranged the funeral then?' This was what she and Sylvia had advised him *not* to open with, but Ellie didn't blame him for being angry.

Debbie frowned. 'Pardon?' She shifted in her seat.

'Weren't you sorting the funeral out with the vicar?'

'We weren't there about that.' Beneath the studied calmness of Ben's voice, there were hints of something else. 'We went about a different matter.'

Finn turned to Sylvia, who was loading mugs onto a tray.

'Perhaps I got that wrong,' she said. 'Sorry. Senior moment. I must've assumed.'

'So, you weren't discussing funeral arrangements?'

'We were not.' Ben answered again.

'OK. That's got things off to a cracking start.' Ellie sensed there was more to come on this. 'Finn? Do you want to ask Debbie about the will?'

Debbie flushed pink and wriggled in her seat.

Finn stared at his aunt. 'You said you didn't know if Mum had a will. You *did* know. You were here when she told us she was revising the one she made two years ago. Why did you lie?'

Debbie threw her husband a sideways glance. 'I had a moment of poor judgement.'

Finn snorted. 'That's not good enough.'

Ellie could see Finn trying to control himself.

'What do you mean?' He wasn't going to let it go.

Sylvia slid the tea tray onto the table and sat down quietly.

Again, Debbie shifted in her seat. 'I wasn't sure what I felt about her changing her will.'

'So you lied about her having one?'

'Essentially, yes. I was considering challenging the new will and wanted to buy some time.'

'You what?' Finn's eyes were blazing. 'I can't believe I'm hearing this.'

'I'm sorry.'

'That's not good enough either. I didn't ask Mum to make me a beneficiary. I didn't know she had until now. And you wanted to prevent me from getting the money? To prevent Mum's will from being carried out?'

Debbie's head was lowered, and when she looked up, tears brimmed in her eyes. 'Yes. Like I said, for a few mad days.'

'And what? You've suddenly had a change of heart?'

'Actually, yes. It was easier when I didn't really know you. When I was angry with you. But over the last few days, I've seen you a few times, and I've had people telling me what a decent young man you are and how you deserve a chance.'

'Good grief,' Sylvia muttered.

'But why? Did you want to punish me? Was that it? I can't believe I'm hearing this.'

Debbie shook her head. She pulled a piece of loo roll from her sleeve and dabbed at her face.

'You might as well tell them, love,' Ben said. He reached out and took his wife's hand. 'Or I can, if you like?'

She nodded.

'I can tell you why. It's not my wife's fault. It's mine. I put her up to it.'

So this was why she'd brought him.

His voice was shaking now. 'I suggested Debbie challenge Andrea's will to pay off my debts.' He paused. 'I am a gambler. No, I'm not just a gambler. I have a gambling *addiction*.' He leant over and took a mug of tea from the tray. Deposited two large spoons of sugar into it and stirred. 'Without my wife knowing, I've run up huge debts. It's true that I was made redundant. But that's not why we've had to sell the bikes. It's because I owe around fifty thousand pounds, and I was hoping we could avoid having to sell the house.'

There was silence around the table.

Ellie clenched her fists to stop herself from jumping in. She was trying to leave Finn to handle the conversation, with people there to support him.

'Just how much persuasion did it take to get you on board with this plan?' Finn fired the question at Debbie.

'I'm really sorry, Finn.' Debbie had her face in her hands.

'Answer the question.'

'I can answer it,' Ben replied. 'A lot. My wife didn't want to challenge the will and said so repeatedly. But I kept on at her. And as the bills mounted, and we've been given ultimatums by the banks, she reluctantly agreed.'

'And would you have told me if you hadn't been rumbled, *Auntie Debbie*?'

Debbie moved her hands from her face. 'I don't know. I honestly don't know.' She looked directly at Finn. 'I knew I had made a wrong decision but I didn't know what to do.'

'So you did nothing?'

'I think I was probably hoping I wouldn't have to do anything, that I could get away with it. Challenge the will, get the money, pay off Ben's debts and–'

'...carry on living like nothing happened?'

She shrugged. 'Yes and no. More like, live with what I'd done.'

'What did you hope to achieve by "buying time"?' Ellie couldn't help herself. She could see that Finn was trying to process what he'd heard. 'Time to do what?'

'To think about how to challenge the will.'

Sylvia cleared her throat. 'What basis were you hoping to use?'

'Her illness,' Ben replied.

'Meaning you planned to claim she was of unsound mind?'

'I'm ashamed to say it, but yes. I'm really sorry, Finn.'

Finn's chair screeched as he pushed it back on the wooden floor. 'Un-flippin-believable.' He got to his feet and stomped across the room towards the door, followed by Zoe.

'I assume you're no longer planning to challenge the will?' Sylvia asked.

'That's correct,' said Ben.

Something was bothering Ellie. 'Is this why you've been so down on Finn? So you could claim he's cashed in and didn't care about his mother?'

'I was planning on including that, yes. But I wasn't making that part up and would have said it anyway. I did feel that way for a long time. My sister didn't find life easy.

She tried her best to bring Finn up without any input from his dad. I'm not saying it was Finn's fault, but he did make that more difficult, and I have been annoyed about that for a long time. And she *was* scared of him.'

'This is a conversation for another time, and one for you and Finn, but the situation was *not* of his making.' Sylvia spoke plainly. 'And let's not forget, he was a child and a teenager, and Andrea was the adult the whole time. She was his *mother*.'

'Of course.'

Ellie felt conflicted. She felt for Debbie but – was that it? Was that all she had to say?

It was as if Debbie had been flattened. She stared at her husband, blinking very slowly, and said, 'I'd like to go now.'

And five minutes later, they had gone. They had literally come, dropped their bombshell and left.

Chapter 28

11.45am

The meeting with Debbie and Ben had left them all in shock. None of them had had the faintest inkling of Ben's debts. The news certainly raised questions about Debbie's motives.

Ellie was back in her jeep, zipping along the coast road towards the village. A watery sun was low in a brooding grey sky. On her left, waves danced and rolled in the thundering grey mass of the sea, oblivious of the snow that had fallen overnight. A ship lay on the horizon, heading for Dover. Snow was coming down again.

Once she rounded the corner into the village, Wootton Castle came into view. The Tudor artillery fort always stood out ... but something wasn't right.

Police lights were flashing.

The bright yellow of an ambulance.

Four yellow, blue and white police cars.

Ellie pulled over at the kerb.

What had happened?

Her thoughts ran to Sue. Her locked premises. The phone going to voicemail. 'I'm really scared,' she'd said.

Then she saw Dave's unmarked car and a crime scene vehicle.

A uniformed officer was tying blue and white tape to the black metal railings. Tall, rangy build. It was Jimmy White from one of the local villages.

She lowered her window.

Jimmy saw her. 'Alright, Mrs Blix?' His expression was grave. He wound the crime scene tape round the painted railings, stretched it and knotted it.

On the ground there was a child's woolly hat that must've been forgotten. On the gate post, a snag of red material was flickering in the wind.

Had someone been killed?

Ellie was processing the shock when Dave trudged up the stone steps from the castle moat, his face ashen, holding Sue and Alan's liver-and-white spaniel on a makeshift lead.

Chapter 29

12pm

Ellie left Wootton Castle in a daze. All Dave would confirm was that it was Sue who had been found, not her husband. Their dog, Lily, had been swabbed and her collar and lead taken for tests, and Dave had asked Ellie to take her while they contacted Sue's husband. What on earth had happened? It was clear the police thought Sue had died in suspicious circumstances. Questions darted through Ellie's mind. She had been due to collect Sue, but she hadn't been there. How had she ended up dead at the castle?

Ellie needed to clear her mind. She didn't have to meet Finn until 2pm, so she decided to take the dogs for a run. With Brian Silk in mind, she told Sally where she was going and checked the battery on her personal alarm.

Five minutes later, she was on local Hawking Down, the disused WW1 airfield. The miles of open fields were one of her favourite walking spots. Ellie strode purposefully, hands in her pockets, her eyes down. The falling snow was returning yesterday's grey slush on the plateau of chalk grassland to a pure, white blanket. Cold flakes of snow landed on her cheeks. As she walked, she was deep in thought, absorbing the shocking awfulness of another death. Thank goodness for this place, which she knew so well. She found it comforting that the vast open space allowed her thoughts to wriggle free and was grateful that each step shook them into place a little bit more.

In the distance, ships chugged along their route in and out of Dover, just as they did every day of the year. In their sleepy little village though, everything was far from normal, and now there had been another suspicious death.

First Andrea, now Sue.

The two had to be linked, surely?

In the grey sky above, the moon was contemplating making an early appearance. On the ground, Rebus was somersaulting and barking and zooming about in the snow with Sue's dog, Lily, both apparently oblivious of the tragedy that had just landed on the village. A few yards away, three rabbits bobbed back into the safety of the bramble bushes.

In the ravages of Ellie's mind, questions reared their heads. What had Sue been scared of? Where had she gone, after phoning Ellie? If only Ellie had got to the bistro earlier.

As Ellie walked, she relished the cold air on her face. Time passed. Fifteen or twenty minutes, she wasn't sure. The snow was coming down heavily now and it was getting more difficult to see. A lurcher slowly came into focus, bounding across the snow, zig-zagging this way and that, yellow bandana flapping in the wind. It was Oscar, Martha's dog. He was in full flight, legs at their furthest reach, making quick progress over the field towards the old aerodrome. Had he gone after a rabbit?

Ellie scoured the scene, expecting Martha to come into view. Where was she? Ellie was trying to rein in her imagination, to tell herself that Brian Silk was a stalker. As far as she knew, he didn't attack women on walks. Did he?

'Oscar,' she called. 'Here boy.' She fished in her pockets for treats. Called Rebus and Lily back to her so there would be other dogs for Oscar to run to.

Ellie carried on calling the lurcher, making her voice as encouraging and friendly as she could. He was closer now, still bounding through the thick snow, drunk on freedom and at the mercy of his instincts. Eventually, Rebus and Lily ran towards him, barking and leaping, and a few moments later, Oscar skidded to a halt.

'Good boy.' Ellie stepped off the path into the snow on the field. Immediately, she sank into a drift. The crisp snow swallowed her boots and came up to her knees. Aware she needed to be careful, she waded over to Oscar and clipped Rebus' lead on his collar before he took off again. Then she checked the battery on her mobile. Four bars. She was OK. 'Let's find your mum, eh boy?'

Ellie's heart was thumping in her chest.

She looked back to where she'd come from, studying the scene in front of her. She could just make out the hedgerow that ran along the path up from the car park. In the blue, snowy light, other than Oscar's panting, there were no sounds and no sign of movement. Thank goodness she'd caught the dog. There had been two deaths, and despite her attempts to calm herself, Ellie felt jumpy. Sylvia's comments kept coming into her mind, and she found it hard not to imagine Martha's body lying in the bushes. What if Martha's protectiveness towards Andrea had thwarted Silk in some way? Enraged him and made him come after Martha? Where on earth *was* she?

They all headed along the path in the direction of where Oscar had first appeared. It was still light, but with heavy snow clouds moving across from the east, and thick snow, visibility was continually fading.

After a few minutes, in the distance, Ellie heard a faint voice. A woman's, shouting, 'Oscar, *Oscar*, come.'

It was Martha.

'I've got him,' Ellie yelled back. 'Martha? Where are you?'

Slowly, a figure emerged from the path out of a copse. *Thank goodness*. But something wasn't right. Her head was down. She was moving slowly and limping. Had she had a fall – or been hurt?

'Martha, over here.' Ellie shouted and waved, hoping the woman would see her and know she was safe now.

For a few moments, Martha didn't seem to hear. Then she looked up. She must've seen Ellie and the dogs in the distance as she briefly raised her arm ... and then dropped to the ground like a deflated balloon.

Ellie grabbed her phone from her pocket. Dave would be busy. Pete? That seemed a bit cheeky. She dialled Finn.

'Mrs Blix?' he answered.

'Someone's injured on Hawking Down. Is there any chance you could help me?'

'Yeah, sure. I'll come now.'

'I've got her dog, but the woman's limping, and the snow's really thick up here. It's Martha.'

'Ah.' He stopped. 'In that case, no.'

Ellie felt her patience drain away.

'Sorry. I'll get someone else.'

Ellie heard a voice in the background.

'She's on the downs,' Finn whispered.

'Let me speak to her,' Ellie heard.

There was rustling, then Zoe came on. 'Mum? I'm calling Dad.'

Ellie caught the fear in her daughter's voice.

'Where the heck are you? Have you forgotten about Brian Silk?'

'In the field between the old airfield, Hawking Down Road and the beach. I'll join Martha and stay with her. Tell Dad we'll be in the south-east corner of the field, by the road. Keep an eye out for three dogs and two people. If Martha needs an ambulance, I'll call one when I get to her.'

'OK. Stay with Martha,' Zoe told her. 'Dad can come round the beach road and get you. It'll be much quicker than walking over the downs in the snow.'

She rang off. A few minutes later, Ellie reached Martha, who by this time had got to her feet and hobbled to a bench.

'Hey. So glad you're safe.'

'Oscar took off, and I twisted my ankle running after him.' Martha's voice was weary and she was trembling. She bent over and rested her hand on her injured foot.

Oscar tugged at his lead, desperate now to get back to his owner.

'Hang onto him, Ellie, could you? He's a little so-and-so. He'll be off again.'

Ellie sat down next to her. 'I was really worried back there. We couldn't see you for ages.'

She checked Martha over for obvious signs of injury. 'Is it just your ankle?'

Martha was wincing. 'Hopefully. Although I landed awkwardly and my shoulder isn't great.' She forced a weak smile. 'Thank goodness you were up here. I was so rude to you last time I saw you. I wouldn't have blamed you if you'd left me here.' She laughed. 'That'll teach me to come out without my phone.'

'Dave's coming to get us, if he's able to get away. Zoe's ringing him.' Ellie was aware he'd probably be furious with her for dragging him away from the crime scene. 'You won't have heard, then. Sue's been found at the castle. There's been another death.'

'Sue's *dead*? I heard the sirens. What happened? I've been up here for ages.'

'Don't know yet. The castle is taped off.'

Now that Ellie was seated, tiredness clawed at her. Finn's voice entered her head, and before she knew it, she'd opened her mouth. 'I asked Finn if he'd come and help us. It was very strange. He agreed immediately, but when I said it was you, he refused.' The beginning of a question was forming in her mind.

Martha stared at Ellie for a few moments, blinking.

'Why would he have done that?'

'No idea. Maybe he was busy.'

But that didn't make sense. He'd said he'd come, and then changed his mind. Ellie let her question ride the air for a few moments before asking gently, 'Do you not get on with Finn?'

'I don't really know him. We've met several times, obviously, at Andrea's over the years, but I've never had much to do with him. I've always struggled with the distress he caused his mum. Maybe he's picked up on that?'

Ah. That made sense. It was Martha's protectiveness again.

'Andrea's become like a sister to me over the years.'

A car engine distracted Ellie.

'When my son died, I wanted a change of scene, a fresh start.'

A door slamming.

'Moving here and meeting her has been life-changing for me.'

Voices. Shouting. Thank goodness. They were safe.

Chapter 30

1pm

At the police station, Dave led Ellie into one of the soft interview rooms. The walls were a scruffy white, and it was sparsely furnished, just two boxy sofas and a coffee table on a hard floor.

'Here you go.' He handed her a cup of vending machine tea and a mini-packet of bourbon biscuits.

Ellie took the cup and biscuits and sat down.

'What on earth were you playing at with Katie Douglas?' Dave could hardly conceal his annoyance. 'She rang me and asked if you were our prime suspect. Started on about lab analyses.'

'Sorry.' Ellie unzipped her coat and slipped it off. Her boots were still covered in snow and mud from the downs. She told him what Katie had said about him having an affair. 'I saw red.'

'It's a double murder investigation, for goodness' sake. You can't go around making up things that could materially affect–'

'It was stupid of me. I'm really sorry. I thought if I pretended to know what the poison was in, I'd get it out of her. I did. I know it was in Andrea's tea.'

'How did you know she was poisoned?'

'I heard you mention it on the phone the other day.'

'You've got to stop this. Going over to Andrea's was bad enough. Next time, I'll make sure you're nowhere near me when I'm having work conversations.' He paused. 'You never did any of this when we were together. I always trusted you not to interfere.'

'Yes, well, trust went out of the window last Christmas when I learnt about your affair.'

For a moment, Dave's face tightened. Gradually it softened again. 'I'm tempted to say that you only have yourself to blame for the *Gazette* article. Goodness knows who's read it. Maybe it'll teach you a lesson about meddling in police investigations.' He settled himself on the sofa adjacent to hers. His face was a mass of stubble and lines, and he had dark rings round his eyes. 'At least we've got your prints and DNA to eliminate, *finally*. And your statement.'

Ellie sighed.

There was a gentle lilt to his voice. He'd agreed to come and collect Martha and Ellie and the dogs if she agreed to come into the station afterwards.

'Next time you want to get lost in the snow, could you do it when someone has *not* just been murdered, and when there isn't a stalker in the area?' He brushed mud off his suit trouser legs.

Ellie was about to say that she hadn't got lost and it was Zoe who'd rung him, not her – but she was exhausted and couldn't be bothered to argue. Plus – something else was bothering her. She'd been in Dave's flat, of course, and seen him outside the oast house when she was cleaning, but it was a long time since she'd seen his face this close up, met his eyes with hers, and it was simultaneously comforting and unsettling. He looked shattered. Getting older, like her, she supposed.

'Right.' He pulled his notepad out. 'What *exactly* did Sue say to you this morning?' He took the top off his biro.

Ellie repeated their conversation.

'She *actually* said she was really scared?'

'Uh-huh.' She cast her mind back. 'First, would I come with her, then, that she was scared.'

'Was she scared about coming here to the station, do you think? Or was she scared about something else, and she wanted you to come for moral support?'

Ellie paused to think. 'Moral support, definitely. From her actual words, it might seem like she was anxious about what you might ask her. And maybe she was. But I got the impression it was more that she had something to tell you. And, whatever it was, it was burdening her.' She sat back and thought further. 'For example, she double-checked I'd meet her. I may be wrong but the sense I got was that she was worried about something she *knew* or had *seen*.'

Dave was nodding.

'There's something else though.' She told him about her conversation with Jane at the hair salon.

Dave jotted a few notes on his pad. '"He doesn't want to"? No mention of who that referred to?'

Ellie shook her head. 'That it? Can I go now? Sue's spaniel will probably be chomping his way through my car seats.' She was about to stand up.

Dave put his hand out and quickly drew it back in. 'Finn said you guys had a chat.'

'That's right.' She hadn't anticipated him wanting to talk about family things while he was on duty. 'Actually, I need to ask you something. Two things, in fact.'

'*Ellie.*' The warning tone in his voice was unmistakeable.

'They relate to Zoe.'

He sat back with a thump.

'Where is Brian Silk? I'm worried about Zoe, with a stalker on the loose. Sylvia said–'

'Mum? God help us.' Dave placed his hand on his forehead. 'Don't tell me you've got my mother involved with this sleuthing nonsense of yours?'

'Funny you thought it was my idea. Where is Silk?'

'We don't know. We're still trying to locate him.'

'Is he a suspect for Andrea's mur–?'

'Nice try. You know I cannot tell you. What's the other thing?'

'Can you let me know when you find him?'

'When I'm allowed to.'

'OK. Debbie Burdett told me that Andrea was scared of Finn. Do we need to be worried about him being violent with Zoe? I asked him about it and he downplayed it. You know more about that side of him from before he left town.'

Dave sat up straight. 'I've asked him about it too. He *was* physical around Andrea. Like, he'd slam doors and stomp about. And he kept getting into fights with peers. But he was never violent *towards* her. At least, not that she ever mentioned.'

'If he hurts Zoe...'

'He won't. I'll make sure of that.'

His eyes were on hers, and his expression was so gentle, so tender, Ellie got butterflies in her stomach.

For a few brief moments, the room stood still, and Ellie realised she was holding her breath.

'Ellie, I'm sorry about the other day. Look. I need to tell you something.' Dave's voice was only just audible.

Ruby.

Dread glugged in Ellie's stomach. This was it. He was in a new relationship.

'I know why Andrea got back in touch with you. She told me.'

Wait. He knew?

There was a sharp knock on the door and a uniformed officer burst in. 'Guv, you're needed.'

Ellie knew that look.

'*Urgently.*'

Chapter 31

1.30pm

'Who are your suspects then?' Sally's voice was a bit muffled.

Organ music reverberated round the vast white vestibule of the Chapel of the Sacred Heart in Lower Wootton.

'Do you think the same person killed Andrea and Sue?'

The two women were arranging flowers for the Christmas services. Sally pushed a white lily into the huge stone vase. It nestled next to pine branches and long-stemmed red roses. 'Mmm. These smell *gorgeous*.' She sank her nose into the display to get a better smell.

Ellie groaned. 'There are too many suspects. Some have possible motives, others are on the list because their behaviour seems suspicious.' She added a eucalyptus branch to the display. Sunlight streamed through the stained-glass windows onto the wooden pews and the red-and-black tiled floor. A bright, white cloth covered the altar. 'Sue was one because she had issues with Andrea, but she's obviously off the list now. However, I'm certain that her murder is linked to Andrea's, and she was clearly scared.'

'Oh?'

'What of, I'm not sure yet. Let's start with Finn's dad, Luke. He wasn't happy about Andrea asking him to involve Finn in his life and will.'

'Pete and I caught an episode of *The Canterbury Murders* last night. He's rather charismatic, isn't he?'

'Yes. He is. And Andrea was pushing for Finn to know that Luke's his dad.'

'Woah.' Sally stopped what she was doing. 'I'd say that that's a pretty strong set of motives right there. Wouldn't you? The mother of the child you've never had anything to do with, and about whom your current wife and children know nothing, suddenly wants you to step up and be Daddy?'

'Yup. Except – come on. He's on the telly. However annoyed he might be in private, is he really going to risk his career by bumping her off?' She recalled what Debbie had told her about his various properties. 'I suppose men like him probably pay other people to do their dirty work.'

She'd been trying to think of ways to find out more about him. Meet him even.

'Who else?'

'Andrea had a stalker from her acting days. He's just come out of prison...'

Sally gasped.

'... and he's broken the terms of his licence and absconded.'

'You're kidding?'

'He's been in contact with Andrea and he's been skipping his meetings with his probation officer. Dave said they're trying to find him.'

'He's got to be a suspect then. He sounds dangerous. I'm going to rethink where I walk Luna.'

'Definitely worth being careful. I've asked Zoe to be.' She altered the position of some of the stems. 'Then there's Debbie, who lied about not knowing whether her sister had a will.' She told Sally about Ben's gambling debts.

'What if she's still lying?' Sally asked. 'Did she seem remorseful? Desperate people do desperate things. Those debts give her a strong motive. Maybe she didn't want to wait for her sister to die naturally?'

'I agree. There's something else. She's clearly not keen on Finn. I can't figure out if that's relevant to Andrea's death.'

'Hmm. Well, having Finn as a co-beneficiary is bound to have increased her antagonism if she wanted the money for herself. Are you sure she's over that?'

'No, I'm not, but she says some of it was about not really knowing Finn, and feeling angry about the ways he made Andrea's life difficult.'

'The two of them will have to get to know each other and work that out.' Sally was typically pragmatic.

'Then, of course, there's Martha. Why would she say she didn't know Andrea before she moved here, when there's a photograph of the two of them together with their babies?'

'Well, she doesn't know that we've seen that photo, so she's probably thinking it's a lie she can get away with.' Sally was always a brilliant devil's advocate. 'If she's still not over her son's death, perhaps she wants to shut down all possibility of being asked about it? So, she doesn't mention knowing Andrea before she came to Wootton.'

'Except someone else – apart from us – must know how and when the two of them met. We are going to have a chat with Bob from school. See if he remembers anything. Zoe tracked him down.' Ellie trimmed a few roses and cut a slit vertically up their stems. 'The other thing I haven't considered is where is the father of Martha's child? Was she married to him? That's another person who must have useful information.'

'Ah. Now. We read the novel, *After You Left,* at book club a few months ago. Martha was there that week, and when we were all chatting about it, she mentioned that she had got divorced just after she had her baby. Her ex-husband lives near Sandwich, I think.'

'Perhaps that's what she and Andrea had in common. Both effectively single mothers.' Ellie's mind was racing. Her stomach gave a rumble. Apart from the biscuits at the police station, she hadn't eaten since breakfast. 'What are you doing later? It's pizza night at the bistro. Do you fancy going?'

'I... I'm ... not sure.' Sally tucked her hair behind her ear in a furtive gesture.

A memory darted through Ellie's mind. 'I knew there was something I was going to ask you about. What was that giggling I heard when I rang you this morning? Have you and Pete *finally* got together?'

Sally blushed. Shrugged. 'Might have.'

'Woo hoo! About flippin' time. This definitely calls for a celebration. Do you and *Pete* fancy a pizza this evening then?'

Sally grinned. 'I'll text him.' She got her phone out, sent a quick message, and put it back in her pocket. 'Right. Back to your suspects. We've got Luke, Martha, Debbie and Brian Silk. Did they all know about her diagnosis?'

'Luke did. Obviously, Debbie did.'

'What about Martha?'

'I assumed that's why she was so protective of Andrea. I know Sue's dead, but her murder is linked to Andrea's, I'm sure of it, and she clearly knew something was up with Andrea because she commented on her inability to learn lines. As for Silk, I've no idea.'

She rotated the stone vase pensively. 'We've done a good job. Looks lovely. Tell your new lover...' she pulled a teasing face, '... his flowers are top notch.'

'Will do.' Sally adjusted the position of the vase. 'Do you think the same person killed Andrea and Sue? It sounds like you had Sue as a suspect for Andrea's murder.'

'I did. And was wondering if we have two killers.'

'And?'

'My gut instinct tells me it's the same person, and Sue was killed because of something she knows. What do you think?'

'Don't know. It sounds possible. We've covered motives. What about the means? By the way, I can't imagine DI-Dave was pleased about you talking to Katie Douglas.'

'Oh, God. Don't.'

'Thought you'd learnt your lesson about her after that hatchet job she ran on you?'

'Apparently not.'

'So, who could have put thallium in Andrea's tea?'

'I don't know yet. There's no issue around supply. Thallium's easy enough to get hold of. As for who added it and how to prove it – the Blix women are on the case.'

'I'm sure DI-Dave will be thrilled to know that.'

Ellie grinned. At that moment her phone rang. 'Sylvia. How's it going?'

'You might want to sit down,' Sylvia told her. 'I've tracked down Luke McKenzie. I literally know where he is today, right at this moment.'

Ellie nearly dropped her phone. She yelled to Sally, 'She's only flippin' found Finn's dad.'

'Where is he?' Sally bounded over to Ellie. 'Put her on loudspeaker.'

'I thought it was about time I joined social media,' Sylvia continued. 'I know. Don't laugh. But Zoe and Finn are constantly finding out about things on there, so I joined Twitter. Finn doesn't know who his dad is yet and neither does Zoe, so I've been trawling through all the 'Luke McKenzie's on there and eventually found his account. He is filming a trailer in Canterbury today for the new series of *The Canterbury Murders*. In Westgate Gardens.'

Ellie was momentarily speechless.

'Shall we pay him a visit?'

She caught the mischief in Sylvia's voice.

Ellie had arranged to meet Finn at the school. 'Oh, heavens. I've got a million and one cleaning jobs.' She was racking her brains for what she could move around, but she'd only been through that process a few hours earlier when Laura had rung. 'I don't think I can.'

'I can go.' Sally was practically jumping up and down. 'Is he definitely there?'

'Yes. He's just tweeted a photograph of himself with his co-lead. The blonde woman who was DI Banks' sergeant on ITV.'

'That's fine,' Sally said. 'We can drive. Sylvia, I'll pick you up in ten minutes.'

Things were moving so fast, Ellie's head was in a spin. And something that Sylvia had said was bothering her. 'Hang on. Before you go – are Zoe and Finn within hearing distance?'

'No. They're upstairs in Zoe's bedroom.'

'I should've thought about this before. Finn needs to know who his father is. I haven't had the chance to talk to Debbie about it yet. I don't want Zoe telling him and have him charge off to Canterbury, screaming at his dad. It needs to be done properly. And we can't tell Zoe who he is and ask her to keep secrets from Finn. It's not fair.'

'Oh, no. I'm not going to like this, am I?'

'We're going to *have* to keep it from both of them for a bit longer.'

'Ellie. You were furious about them–'

'I know. I'm being a hypocrite. But hopefully it will just be for another day. Then, we *have* to tell him. And I will take responsibility. I will tell him it was my decision. Don't worry.'

'OK. But only if it's one more day. It would be dreadful if he finds out and we've kept it from him.'

Chapter 32

2pm

It was early afternoon in Westgate Gardens in Canterbury. Sylvia and Sally were standing on the path by the bank of the Stour. Ducks stood in huddles, occasionally pecking at the snow-covered ground.

'That's Luke McKenzie. Under the weeping willow by the wall.' Sylvia intended to whisper but she was so excited she couldn't keep her voice down. 'I've never been to a film set. Have you?'

'Sshh. No,' Sally hissed back at her. 'Act natural. We're simply out feeding the ducks and having a nice walk.'

'In the freezing snow?'

'Yes. Well. We're peri- and post-menopausal.'

Sylvia giggled. 'Cheeky mare.' She took in all the filming paraphernalia. The lights and crew. The catering van, the portaloos, the trailers. 'Blimey. It must be like organising a circus.'

Sally chuckled. 'Do you know what you're going to say to him?'

'I think so.' Sylvia took her notebook out of her bag and turned to a fresh page.

'We're lucky. There don't seem to be too many security staff.' Sally surveyed the set. 'Probably because of the snow. The place is deserted. Now. We're likely to have a few seconds to make contact. If he doesn't bite, and we're spotted, we'll be escorted away.'

'Let's go.'

The two of them moseyed onto the set, smiling and giggling like a couple of schoolgirls. They headed straight for Luke McKenzie and his female counterpart.

'Mr McKenzie?' Sally called. 'My mum is ever such a big fan of your program. Could she get your autograph?'

Sylvia pretty much skipped over to him. 'I am. I really am. The river. The marshes. The beautiful wildlife. And the plots. I love how they evolve naturally from Kentish traditions and ways of life. How lovely to meet you. This is my–'

'...daughter,' said Sally. 'Pleased to meet you. Mum would love it if you'd sign her–'

Sylvia shoved her notebook and pen at him. It was the pad she used for her shopping lists.

Luke's female colleague drifted away and left him to it.

'Of course. Your name is...?'

'Sylvia. Thank you. That's so kind. We won't keep you.'

The paper flapped in the wind while Luke tried to scribble his signature.

'We were just having a lovely walk. Came across you quite by chance.' Sylvia stared at Sally, momentarily lost for words.

'Yes. Walking. The ducks. Mum likes to get her ten thousand steps in.' She gave an exaggerated eye-roll at Luke, realising she was talking gibberish.

'Really?' he said. 'Me too. Have you seen the heron round the next corner? He always sits on the reeds. Such noble creatures.'

'Ah, that's lovely. Actually, I think we have a few things in common. Finn Burdett? Your son? He would love to see you. Why won't you see him?'

Luke looked startled. 'Who are you? What are you doing here?'

'He really would like to see you. Especially now his mum's dead. Why won't you?'

'I've been told for years now that he didn't want to see me. But I have no idea who you are, and I really don't see what business it is of yours.' He looked to the left and right and waved his arm. 'Security! I need some help here.'

Within seconds, two burly men arrived – just as Sally had said they would – and escorted them off the set, while Sylvia apologised profusely.

They hadn't even crossed the wooden bridge over the river when Sylvia whispered, 'What do you make of that? He's either a complete liar, or someone's poisoned him against Finn.'

Chapter 33

2pm

By the time Finn arrived at Wootton Primary School, Ellie had wiped the snow off the wall by the main entrance and was perching on the cold stone, stuffing the last bite of her sandwich into her mouth. All around the pretty yellow brick building, snow covered every surface: the children's plant pots by the doors, the playground, the school roof. A trail of grit led to the entrance. The caretakers must have been.

'Alright?' Finn asked.

'Yup. Thanks for giving me a hand.' She wiped crumbs away from her mouth.

'Shocking about Sue.' His eyes searched Ellie's face and he lowered his voice. 'D'you think it's related to Mum's death?'

'That's my guess. Before I forget, I need to ask you something.'

'Go for it.'

'The thallium that killed your mum was in a cup of tea in her bedroom.' She told him about the police finding it in the dregs that were left.

'You're kidding?'

'No. She must've drunk enough for it to kill her but not quite finished it all. Thallium is slow-acting, so she might have drunk the tea two or three days before she developed symptoms. Kathy from the bakery said your mum had stomach pains before the carols when they went out for tea. Now, I'm asking everyone who's been in the house. Please can you compile a list of anyone in that time period who either made your mum a cup of tea, or could have? What we need to find out is who could have put thallium in it.'

'Sure. But I wasn't with her 24/7. She went out quite a few times and I nipped out to meet Zoe.'

'So, who came into the house in that period?'

Finn seemed to be sifting through his memory. 'Kathy dropped off a cake. Sue came round. Martha popped round a few times. The cleaner was there for a couple of hours. Debbie. Bob helped Mum with a burst pipe. That's about it, I think.'

'OK.' Ellie noted the names in her phone. 'We haven't spoken to Bob yet. Maybe you and Sylvia could do that?'

'No problem. I'll arrange it.'

'Can you try and pinpoint who came on which day and roughly what time? And let me know? For example, did it coincide with, I don't know, the news or a phone call or a meal?'

'Will do.'

'Thanks.' Ellie also wanted to ask Finn about Martha, but she sensed it was less challenging if she posed the question as they worked. 'I'll show you what we're doing in each room.' Ellie let them in and led Finn through the reception area and into a classroom. On the door it said, 5F – Miss Henderson. 'Oof, warm in here. They must've forgotten to turn the heating down when term ended.' She removed her coat, scarf and jumper.

Opposite her, Finn had taken his coat off too.

'In every classroom, we empty the bins, wipe all surfaces and hoover the floor. I clean the inside of the windows once a week but we won't do that today. If you start over there,' she pointed at the other side of the room, 'we can do them together.' She sprayed a table and wiped it.

'I came here.' Finn was smiling. He strode over to the window and peered out, surveying the playground. 'I always loved the swings. Pestered Mum for a whole year to get one for the garden at home.'

It was the first time Ellie had heard Finn call the Priest House 'home'.

'She gave in eventually and Uncle Bob put one up.' His expression was wistful. 'Think she got sick of me asking.'

Ellie laughed.

Finn pulled off his hoodie and chucked it into the corner on top of his coat. He took a cloth and some spray from Ellie's cleaning basket and began wiping the tables. He threw his energy into his work and moved quickly from one table to the next. 'Zoe's feeling better today. Her temperature's gone.'

'That's great.' Ellie had spoken to her daughter earlier and knew this, but was happy for Finn to chat away.

'I don't like temperatures. They scare me.' He sprayed and wiped in a circular movement. 'She keeps going on about putting decorations up.' He chortled, and his face broke into a warm smile.

'My daughter *loves* Christmas. Always has. I didn't want decorations this year. Really couldn't be bothered. But Zoe got them out of the cupboard, put them up.'

The two of them chatted while they worked and fell into a companionable silence when they started hoovering. They were in the second classroom now.

'Debbie wants to come over later to discuss the funeral,' Finn said gently.

Ellie recalled the woman's comments in the pub about Finn. 'It's nice that you're organising it together.' She paused to see if he wanted to say any more.

'Suppose.'

Ellie moved a pot of pens and a pile of board markers on Miss Henderson's desk.

'It's hard, knowing that Mum used to tell her about every row we had. When Mum kicked me out, Debbie said it was my own fault. I always felt she took Mum's side.' He squirted spray on another table and wiped it.

'That is tough. I guess it's what sisters do. Especially if your mum was struggling.' Ellie paused. 'I'm not defending her. Just playing devil's advocate.'

'I keep trying to show her I'm different. I've changed.'

'She'll accept it. Just might take time. That's all.'

'Guess so.' Finn took the room in. Panelled cupboards along the back wall. Board at the front. Tables in clusters of four. 'This was my old classroom. Miss Atkinson was my teacher.'

'I'm sure she lives in the village still. Helps out at the library now, I think. Curly hair and glasses?'

‘That’s her.’ He chuckled. ‘Loved her lessons. She always put in my reports, “If Finbar concentrated more, he could achieve anything he wanted”.’

‘Ah. That’s nice. Most of us don’t have that ability. And – *Finbar?*’ She laughed. ‘I love it. Think I’ll call you that from now on.’

‘It’s on my birth certificate.’

Ellie decided to ask him about Martha. ‘What do you remember about when you were growing up?’

‘Most of it. Makes me sad to think about though, with Mum gone now.’

Ellie recalled the photograph that she and Sally had found at Martha’s. ‘Did you guys spend much time with Martha and her son?’

Finn stopped. ‘Yeah.’ He stared at Ellie.

‘Can you tell me about it?’

‘You know about Nate, don’t you?’

‘Only that he died. I don’t know any details.’

‘Nate was like a brother to me. Same age. We liked the same things. You and Zoe would have loved him.’

Ellie caught the sadness in his voice. ‘That must have been hard for you.’ She sprayed the desk and wiped it. She was used to the smell, but this time it hit her nostrils. ‘What happened?’

'He developed meningitis when he was thirteen. Actually ... wait a sec.' He put his cloth down and got his phone from his pocket. Swiped the screen alive and tapped at his apps. 'Look.' He held out his battered phone. 'Here he is.' In the browning image, a mousey-haired boy was holding a miniature wooden horse with the tips of his fingers. His face was pure delight. A blond boy was poring over the toy with him, both of them captivated, their faces so close they were touching.

'I made that horse for him.' Finn's voice was thick with love. 'In Uncle Bob's tool shed.' He kept his hand on his heart as though there was an invisible cord. 'We often said we felt more like twins than friends.'

His face softened, as though the memories warmed him. 'Although – he was darker haired than me and had a rosy complexion, and I'm pale and–'

'...blond.' Ellie was scrabbling about in her head for what to say and how to word it. Not only had he been born into 'half a family', he also hadn't had any siblings. And the boy who was the closest he'd had to a brother had been taken from him.

Finn was trembling.

'I can only imagine what it must have felt like to lose him. I'm glad Dave has mentioned counselling and is helping you to get some.'

Finn sniffed and wiped his face with the back of his hand. 'Why did it have to happen to him? He was the kindest, loveliest person in the world.' He paused. 'Not bitter and angry, like me.'

'I don't have an answer for that. I don't think many people who have lost loved ones do.'

Finn was still shaking.

Ellie put her hand on his and gently removed it from his heart. 'It will be OK. I know it isn't now – but it will be. And I know it's not the same, but you have Zoe now. And Sylvia and me. And I know Dave has always cared about you. We will help you to get through this.' She waited. 'And whatever Debbie feels, that can shift. Everything can. Not overnight, but it can change if you want it to.'

Finn flopped. He put his hand out to steady himself. 'Thanks, Mrs B.' He exhaled loudly. 'I can't... I need to...' He stopped. 'Shall I hoover?'

'Before you do that, given we're talking about it, can I ask you about Martha quickly?'

Finn froze.

'Every time I mention her name, you–'

'Freeze?'

'Yes.'

'Zoe said that too.' He was tapping on a desk. 'I just can't stand the woman. That's all.'

'Did something happen?'

Finn plugged in the vacuum cleaner, eager to end the conversation.

'Finn?'

He sighed. 'When Nate died, she kept wanting me to spend time with her. She'd keep asking Mum if she could take me for an ice cream or to the park. Or shopping.'

That was understandable, given she'd lost her son, but... 'You didn't want to?'

'I *definitely* didn't want to. I felt... I don't know ... *uncomfortable*. She would cry for hours and want me to be there to comfort her.' As he stood, his features crumpled, and he looked as though he was imagining how he had felt on those occasions. 'She would put her arms round me and try to stop me from moving and would sob on me.' He shuddered. 'It weirded me out.'

Golly. That did sound strange.

'One time, she took me to the shops and told people she was my mum. How messed up is that?'

'Wow. Very.' Ellie was taking in what Finn was saying. 'What did your mother think about it?'

'She understood. She kept telling Martha, "He doesn't want to". But each time – it made her even more upset.'

'Oh dear. That must've been extremely tough.' Finn's words reminded Ellie of something, but she couldn't put her finger on what it was.

'It was.' He closed his eyes momentarily. 'Anyway, that's enough about all that. Let's get this cleaning finished, shall we?' He switched his hoover on and pushed the extension brush over the carpet in long sweeps. As he hoovered, Ellie watched him. Something had registered in her brain. In the baking classroom, in his T-shirt, his pale limbs shimmered in the weak light. His blond hair covered his face.

Ellie gasped.

That was it.

His pale limbs and blond hair.

'Stay here, finish the cleaning. OK? I've got to go and get something.' Her voice was stern. 'I'll be back to lock up.' She grabbed her car keys and ran for the exit.

Chapter 34

3pm

On the way over to the Old Post Office, Ellie was trying to decide what she'd say if Martha was in. She'd left something behind? Dropped an earring? Lost a contact lens?

Fortunately, when she arrived, there was still no sign of Martha's car. Perhaps she had gone to get her ankle checked out. Ellie would just have to hope she could get in, get a copy of the photograph, and get out without Martha coming home – otherwise she was going to need those excuses.

Ellie let herself in and dashed into the kitchen to switch off the alarm, then ran upstairs to Martha's bedroom. She couldn't hear a sound, so she eased the wardrobe door open and took down the box. It took her a couple of seconds to find the photographs that she and Sally had seen earlier of Martha and Andrea with their babies. She snapped a couple of pictures with her phone. Put the lid back on the box, stowed it back in its place and closed the wardrobe doors. And let out a sigh of relief. She was about to head back downstairs when she heard the front door open.

'Hello-o?' It was Martha. 'Who's here? The alarm's off and–'

'Only us. Blix Blitz.' Ellie tried to sound breezy. 'Just finishing.'

Dammit. Why had she had to come back? Ellie bounded downstairs, heart hammering in her chest like an electric sewing machine. She pulled a friendly smile onto her face. 'That's it. Final checks done. All the windows are locked and taps off. I'm done.'

Martha was staring at her, her eyes and forehead creased with a frown.

'How's your ankle?'

'Not too bad. I'm about to get an ice pack.'

'Oh, great.' Ellie wanted to get away. She pointed at the lounge and jiggled her keys in her palm. 'Mirrors came up lovely. Oh – with Christmas, do you want us next week, or would you prefer to make it two weeks today?'

'Er ... a fortnight's fine.' Martha was rubbing her temples.

And before she could say any more, Ellie shot past her and out the door.

Chapter 35

5pm

Finn finished cleaning at the school. As soon as Ellie had locked up, he went to meet Sylvia so they could go to talk to Ellie's old schoolfriend, Bob Campbell.

It was dark when they got off the bus. Priory Park was a large multi-functional recreation area which ran along the main road a mile out of Little Wootton. Like everywhere else, it was covered by a blanket of snow.

'There's his pickup,' Sylvia said.

The vehicle she was pointing at had 'CAMPBELL TREE SURGERY' on the side. It was off the road on one of the entrances to the park.

'I can't believe we've come all this way in the freezing cold just to ask him if he saw anyone make your mum tea.' Sylvia was enjoying getting to know Finn and she admired his forthrightness.

Finn laughed. 'Not *just* for that reason. He said he had something important to tell us.'

'He better have.'

Bob saw them and waved. In the dark, they could see him clearly because he was standing under floodlights. He switched off his chainsaw and placed it in the back of his pickup. Then he slid his helmet off and put it with the saw. 'It's still really slippery. The path's been gritted so stay there. I'll come to you.' He strode over to meet them, thick boots clomping on the snow. He was over six feet, and with all the layers and pockets in his workwear, it was hard to tell if he was well built or just well insulated.

'I'd love a go with his saw,' Finn told Sylvia.

'Maybe he'll let you one day. Let's find out what he knows. If you want to stay and chat after that, it's up to you.'

'Thanks for coming,' Bob said. 'I've almost finished for the day. We can pop into the changing room if you like. There's no one in there and it's heated.' He steered them towards a single storey building with a corrugated iron roof, chatting as they walked. 'Ellie rang and asked if I'd seen anyone make a cup of tea for Andrea when I was there fixing her pipe.' He opened the door to the changing room, flicked the lights on and they filed in.

'That's better.' Relief filled Sylvia's voice. She had always felt the cold and it was getting worse with age.

The room was lined with lockers, benches and coat racks. It had a faint whiff of stale sweat and damp.

Bob continued talking. 'To start with I couldn't think of anyone because I was outside almost the whole time and at the back of the house. So, anyone could have entered through the front door and I wouldn't have seen them–'

'But...' Finn tried to cut in.

'This is the thing. I went over and over it in my mind. And then I remembered. I *did* go into the house. Andrea had developed a migraine. It was part of her tumour. She had gone to her bedroom and got into bed and forgotten to take painkillers with her. She texted me – I can only think no one else was around – to ask if I could get her tablets from the kitchen and bring them in to her.' He paused and looked at Finn. 'I've known your mum since school, so I thought, well, if she didn't mind me going into her bedroom, I didn't, and she said she was feeling a bit nauseous. Long story short, I took her the tablets and placed them on her bedside table. Idiot that I am, I didn't think about taking a glass of water too, but that was OK because there was a mug of tea there. Next to the tea, there was a set of car keys.'

'Come on,' Sylvia prompted. 'Whose were they?'

'I assumed they were Andrea's. Her clothes were on the floor, so I thought she'd dumped things down in a hurry, desperate to get into bed. I get migraines occasionally and I know what they're like. You literally feel desperate for relief. But, later, when I got home, I realised that the keys weren't Andrea's. They had a distinctive key fob on them which I recognised because I had to move the owner's car once, to deliver a load of logs onto their drive. It was one of those photo key fobs, and had a picture of a liver-and-white spaniel. Lily.'

'Were the keys Sue's or Alan's?'

'Sue's. I know they were hers because I had to move Alan's van too, and his keyring is plain.'

'Goodness. And do you think she gave Andrea the poisoned tea?'

'Can't say for sure but I didn't see any other signs that anyone else had been into the house or into Andrea's bedroom.'

Sylvia was taking in the news.

Sue.

She was dead now, of course, but if she had killed Andrea, it could explain the odd behaviour that Ellie had noticed before Andrea was killed? Sue could easily have walked home and not noticed she'd left her keys until she needed to let herself in. Fetched them later or the next day if Alan was at home to open the door for her. By then, Bob had seen them. Could she have killed Andrea and someone else had killed *her*? If that was the case, the only death they had left to solve was Sue's.

Sylvia thanked Bob for his information.

Finn walked her along the gritted walkway out of the park back to the bus stop and waited with her until the bus came to take her back to the village. He then returned to chat to Bob about chainsaws and tree felling. She couldn't wait to tell Ellie and Zoe what she'd found out.

Chapter 36

5.30pm

In the car, Ellie's thoughts were churning like a washing machine. She didn't have any evidence proving who put the poison in Andrea's tea and when they did it. She was chewing over the list Finn had given her of the people who had visited Andrea in the two days before she died. They hadn't been able to find anything tangible on any of them.

Her phone rang. It was Sylvia, calling from the bus. She was on her way home. Sylvia rattled off what they'd learnt from Bob about Sue's keys being on Andrea's bedside table.

'Oh, blimey. That's a turn-up. Good work. Thanks for letting me know.' There was no doubt those were Sue's keys. Ellie had seen them too. 'It's literally all we've got so far. No one else remembers seeing anything. The last person I've got to call is Caroline, who was cleaning there that day.'

Sylvia was nearly home.

'Make sure you don't duck down any dark alleys. That Silk creep is still at large.' Ellie rang off and dialled Caroline's number. Caroline had been at Andrea's when Kathy had delivered the Black Forest Gateau.

After a few rings she answered. 'Hey, Ellie.'

'Sorry to call in the evening. I need to ask you something.'

'What's up?'

'It's about Andrea Burdett's death. It's a long shot but we're asking everyone who's been there this week. When you were cleaning, did anyone come round and make a cup of tea which they took to Andrea in her bedroom?'

'Oh goodness. Lots of people made tea. I'll have to have a think.'

'There was one day when Bob Campbell was there,' Ellie prompted. 'The tree surgeon. He was fixing her pipe.'

'Actually, yes. Sue.'

'Was that the day he was there or a different day?'

'The same day. I remember because he tramped through the house in his boots. Left snow and mud everywhere.'

Chapter 37

6.50pm

Sue's husband, Alan, was out the back in the kitchen when Ellie arrived at the village bistro. She picked her way round the boxes of vegetables and tins of olive oil and anchovies from the main restaurant room and stuck her head round the door.

'Hi, Alan.' She didn't want to make him jump. 'The waitress sent me through. I'm so sorry about Sue.' She was dreading talking to him. It was bad enough him losing his wife in such a brutal way, but they'd now had two people suggest that Sue could have been the person who poisoned Andrea's tea.

'Oh, Ellie, love. That's kind of you.' He was in chef's clothes and was shuffling across the room, stirring pans of sauce, checking on the oven and reading off the order slips on the counter.

'Pizza night appealed to all of us. We weren't sure whether coming in for a meal was going to be a help or a pain in the proverbial. How are you?'

Alan glanced at her. 'Well, you know.' Stubble clung to his chin and cheeks. His eyes bulged with pain and he looked exhausted. 'I simply want to keep busy.'

'Have the police said what happened?' This was her chance to get information she'd never get from Dave.

'Only that she died in the moat, and death was caused by a blow to the back of her head.' He was holding a large, square, plastic tub of mozzarella and his hands clung to it.

'Do they think she was hit or that she fell and banged her head?'

'They don't know.' He shrugged despairingly. 'I can't take it in. How did she get to the castle? It's in the opposite direction from your place.'

'Do they think she died there or somewhere else?'

'I don't know that either.' He frowned. 'The last she told me, she was going to take the scooter over to your place to–'

'*Scooter?*'

'I got her a scooter for her birthday. She took that.'

Ellie's mind was working overtime. Could it have been a scooter she heard leaving Andrea's the night she died? If so, Sue could've been the person who drove off. 'Sorry. I interrupted you. She took the scooter to mine to...?'

'...yes, to drop something off. Said she'd come straight back to go to the police station with you.'

'And she was definitely going to the windmill?'

'That's what she said.'

'What was she dropping off?' Ellie was trying to think whether she'd seen anything unusual by the door at home.

'I don't know.' Alan paused briefly to run through what his wife had been carrying. 'She had her bag over her right shoulder. In her left hand, she had her mobile and an A4 envelope or a package. Something like that.' Then he went back to his pizza bases and sprinkled grated mozzarella on the tomato sauce.

'Did she get to my place, do you know?'

'That's the thing. I've no idea. She set off and I haven't heard from her since then. Someone...' He covered his eyes. 'Someone must have–'

Ellie held a breath for a few moments and allowed herself to imagine what Alan had stopped himself from saying. That someone had intercepted Sue. She could have agreed to go down into the moat with them, or been lured. 'There's CCTV around the castle. And if she arranged to meet someone, there will be phone records. The police will catch whoever it was.'

'I'm not so sure,' he said, his voice dejected. 'Apparently, there are a few parts of the castle which don't have CCTV. And some of the cameras in the moat have been vandalised.'

'Oh no.'

Ellie felt guilty asking him questions when he was upset and trying to work. 'Sorry. I'm not being nosey. Zoe, Sylvia and I are trying to find out what happened to Andrea, and I'm pretty sure Sue's death is linked to hers.'

He wheeled round to face her. 'Do you think so? Please, ask away. Anything that helps find out who did this.' He chucked a tea towel on the worktop and held his breath.

'There are only a couple of things left to ask. Did Sue go up to Andrea's on the night of the carols? When I got there, someone was leaving on a motorbike or a scooter.'

Alan stopped making pizzas. He was nodding. 'She said she had to get something from Andrea's. No one was in, so she used the spare key that Andrea keeps in the shed. You know what villages are like. Some people don't lock their doors and others leave keys.'

'What did she come back with?'

Alan's face clouded over. 'It was exactly like the thing she was taking over to your place earlier.' He carried on, nodding. 'I'm sure of it.'

'OK. That makes sense.'

Next was the cake. 'Why did Sue send Andrea the chocolate gateau?'

'Before she learnt that Andrea was ill, Sue was annoyed about her not turning up at am dram rehearsals and regularly forgetting her lines. It went on for months. She said a few things to her in the heat of the moment which she bitterly regretted.' He put the pizza dough down on the worktop. 'Unkind things about Finn ... and Andrea's mothering.'

Gemma had been telling the truth then. Ellie knew how hard it must be for Alan to talk about his wife's behaviour, so she didn't mention what she'd overheard in the fish and chip shop.

'That's why I suggested she send Andrea a cake. To say sorry.'

'I wanted to ask how she and Andrea got on. Were they close?'

'Not always but I got the impression they became friends in the last few weeks of Andrea's life. She took Sue into her confidence. Andrea told her about the cancer and said she'd been keeping a journal to record her thoughts, fears, milestones and to document things which happened.'

'Oh?'

'Whatever Sue collected from Andrea's the night she died, she knew it was important and that's what she took over to your place.'

'Blimey. That's huge.' Ellie was processing the information. 'It means that someone could have murdered her for whatever that item was – or for something she knew.' Ellie sank back against the wall of the kitchen. 'Sue told me that she was really scared. Do you know what she was scared of?'

'Yes and no.' Alan's eyes were wide with alarm. 'Someone had been bullying Andrea for years, and it had got much worse in the last few weeks. I suspect that, when Andrea took my wife into her confidence, she told her who it was. And I suspect that *that* person found out that Sue knew and started bullying her too. I also think that–'

'She was killed to protect this person?'

A single tear slithered down Alan's cheek. 'Yes,' he said, his voice full of sadness.

'Last question. Did Sue mention anything about seeing an email on Andrea's computer when she went round there on the scooter?'

'She did. She didn't know why it was up on the screen, but she assumed Finn had read it and got distracted, or something. She felt bad for reading it, but she was curious as to whether it was from Andrea's bully.'

Alan had provided a different picture of his wife from the one that had been developing over the last couple of days. One which was complex and conflicted, and which included Sue genuinely caring about Andrea.

Ellie had known Sue for years. Not well, as she'd been in the year below at school. But it was awful to think she had been killed for what she knew. If she had, Andrea's journal was likely to be of interest to Sue's killer. And that meant she had to find that journal – before someone else did.

Chapter 38

7.10pm

Rebus was at the front door when Ellie let herself into the windmill.

'Hey, boy. Just popping in.' She stroked his head and started hunting for the package that Sue had dropped off. Beside the door were outdoor shoes, a bag of Zoe's, an umbrella, a spare dog lead, a ball thrower.

Ellie scoured the porch. Her olive tree stood in its pot to the left of the door. Round the back of the pot, Ellie saw a Jiffy bag. She snatched it up. Rebus, hearing rustling, soon pushed his nose between Ellie's elbow and her side.

'Not for you, I'm afraid.'

The package was addressed to ELLIE BLIX. Ellie recognised Sue's handwriting from the am dram wallpaper at the village hall. Ellie tore open the seal and slid out the contents. It was a green and pink journal, bound and backed with card. Inside the front cover Ellie saw: ANDREA BURDETT. She was about to have a read when her phone rang in a side pocket of her bag. It was Zoe, ringing from the restaurant.

'Gran's only just arrived.' She didn't bother to say hello. 'She had to have a bath to warm up. Where are you?'

'Had to nip home and get something. I'm on my way now.' Ellie tucked Andrea's journal into her bag.

'I can't get hold of Finn. He's gone completely AWOL.'

Zoe paused, and Ellie heard the worry in her daughter's voice.

'Mum, I've got a bad feeling about this. What if something's happened to him? What if the psycho stalker bloke killed Andrea and has come for Finn?'

Chapter 39

7.15pm

Ellie said goodbye to Zoe with a sense of foreboding. She was tired and hungry, but she couldn't escape the sinking feeling that, given Andrea had been murdered, what if someone was after Finn too?

She was out of breath by the time she entered the dining area of the bistro. Finn still hadn't arrived, but Sally, Pete, Sylvia and Zoe were already at a table. She hurried over to join them, the conversation with Alan still swirling round in her head. 'Still no word from Finn?' She looked at Zoe hopefully.

'Nothing.' Zoe's face was pinched with worry.

Ellie needed to act normally. Pretend everything was fine.

Sally and Pete were sitting next to each other, holding each other's hand under the table and grinning from ear to ear.

'Aww,' Ellie said to the pair. 'How gorgeous. Is this your first public outing as a couple?'

Ellie had known Sally since junior school, and in all that time, she had never seen her friend so happy.

Sally and Pete giggled shyly, giddy with happiness, mirroring each other's body movements.

'*And* – we have another couple who don't need to sneak around any more.' She shifted her attention to Zoe and couldn't stop herself from doing a mini clap.

'Oh, Mumm,' Zoe said, cringing in her seat. 'Stop. At least wait 'til Finn gets here.'

'Let's order some drinks, shall we?' Ellie picked up the menu. 'Prosecco? We can have a toast.'

Ellie was just finishing with the waitress when the door opened and Finn came bowling in.

Thank goodness.

'Sorry, sorry.' He brought with him a whoosh of cold air, and his face was glowing. 'I lost all track of time. I was chatting to Uncle Bob.'

'Have you been with him all this time?' Sylvia asked.

'Yes. He says I can start as his apprentice in the New Year.'

Zoe squealed. 'Yay. That's incredible. You clever thing.'

He took off his coat and slid in beside Zoe.

'Well done,' Ellie said. 'And definitely a call for celebration.'

Ten minutes later, Ellie's table was guzzling their second bottle of prosecco. At intervals, Ellie sneaked a glance over at Zoe, to check how she seemed, and at Finn. Was it tasteless to celebrate when his mum had been killed? This was uncharted territory for them all. None of them had had any experience of murder before.

Ellie was sitting next to Finn on one side and Pete on the other, all facing the wall. Each time the restaurant door opened, she heard the bell ding but didn't see who was coming in. She was deep in conversation with Pete about Christmas trees when the bell went. Ellie heard Sally gasp. Her friend ducked and peered over at Ellie.

'Oh, my word. What are they doing here?' Sally whispered.

Ellie shifted in her chair and got the shock of her life when she saw who had just walked into the restaurant.

'I hope he doesn't recognise Sylvia and me from the film set.'

Martha handed her coat to the waitress and placed the yellow golfing umbrella in the bin by the door. The umbrella was just like the one Ellie had seen at Sue's back gate. Martha had changed out of the jeans she'd been wearing a couple of hours ago and was now wearing a cherry red jersey dress and knee-high black boots. The waitress led the way over to a corner table which had a sign saying RESERVED on it. Martha was still limping and followed the tall, fair-haired man in front of her.

Luke McKenzie slid off his long navy coat, folded it over the back of a chair and sat down on the one next to it, opposite Martha. Navy cotton shirt, corduroy trousers in cream.

Crikey. How was this going to play out? Finn had never met his dad, and as far as Ellie knew, he still didn't know who he was. But what if Luke's name had been mentioned at home when he was growing up? She was thinking of the hushed conversations that adults have sometimes around children, which they think aren't heard.

Luke ran his hands through his mousey-blond hair and picked up the menu.

Ellie wasn't sure whether Martha knew they were being watched, but Luke McKenzie clearly did not. When she watched him on TV, in his detective role, she had noticed that his build was muscular and athletic, just like Finn's.

'Mum?' Zoe whispered. 'What's going on?'

Luke clicked his fingers and gestured to the waitress that he wanted to order. Within seconds, the young woman was at their table, order pad and pen in hand.

Finn was deep in conversation with Pete, but Ellie knew that everything could kick off if Finn realised who Luke was.

Sally joined Pete and Finn's conversation, asking questions to keep Finn occupied.

Ellie's brain struggled to think what to do. They were in a small, confined space and anything could attract either Luke or Finn's attention.

Suddenly, a voice piped up from a neighbouring table, 'Are you that bloke off the telly?' A woman got up and inched past Ellie's table towards Luke and Martha's, becoming more confident by the moment. 'You are, aren't you? You're Luke McKenzie from *The Canterbury Murders*. I recognise your hair.'

Finn froze.

Luke looked up from his conversation with Martha.

'Could I get a selfie?' The woman produced her phone from her pocket.

Finn shifted in his seat. The colour was draining from his face and it was as though all his senses were on red alert. 'Luke McKenzie?' he muttered to himself. 'Luke. McKenzie. Where do I know that name from?'

The selfie woman was parallel with Ellie's table now. 'He's on the telly, love,' she said in passing. 'That'll be why you know him.' She held out her phone to him. 'Could you take a pic of me and my mum with him?' The woman was beckoning to her mother. 'Come on, Mum. Come and have your photo taken with the nice detective.'

Finn got to his feet, as though propelled by an inner force. His face was in a tight frown. He gently pushed the woman's phone away. 'Luke McKenzie?' It was as though he was trying out the name to see if he recognised it. '*Luke McKenzie.*' His voice was louder now.

Luke switched his gaze from the selfie woman to Finn.

'I've heard that name.' Finn was walking over to the corner table. His face looked haunted, as though the strands of a memory were reaching through from his distant past. 'I don't know where I've heard it but I know I have. I'm certain of it.' He stopped. He was in front of Martha's table now. 'It's something to do with my mother, isn't it?' He fixed his eyes on Martha for a few moments and then turned and looked at Ellie. Then spun back round to face Luke. 'You knew my mother, didn't you?'

Luke studied the tablecloth in front of him. Cornered.

'Luke McKenzie. I'm right, aren't I?'

Luke kept his gaze low.

'Look at me, dammit,' Finn demanded. He swivelled round and glanced over at his own table, searching their faces. 'I'm right, aren't I? It's him. Is one of you going to tell me the truth?' He crashed his right fist down on Luke and Martha's table, sending rattling cutlery and crockery into the air. 'LOOK AT ME, DAMMIT. You're my father, aren't you? That's who you are.'

'MUM,' Zoe screamed.

All at once, Ellie's table burst into action. She, Zoe, Sally, Sylvia and Pete all leapt to their feet and descended on Finn.

Luke had pushed his seat back and was leaning into the wall, eyes wide with alarm. Still he didn't speak.

Ellie stretched her arm out to Finn. 'Not like this.'

Finn dodged her and leant over the table.

'Come away.' She held her hand out to him.

'Did you know?' His eyes were blazing at Ellie.

'Only a couple of days ago. *Literally.*'

He shoved an empty chair by its back and looked back at the man who had been absent his entire life. 'What sort of coward are you? The selfish type or are you just *weak*?'

Luke was silent.

Finn turned to Martha. 'And you? What's your story? How long have you been going out for dinner with *my dad*?'

'We've known each other for years.' She flickered a nervous smile. 'Through your mum, actually.'

'Did you want him too then, or was it just me you wouldn't leave alone?'

'Please, Finn. Think what you're doing. A lot of people love you.' Ellie took hold of Finn's arm firmly and guided him away. 'C'mon. Come away.'

Suddenly, Zoe ducked under her mum's arm and flung herself at Finn. 'It's OK. It's OK. Everything's going to be OK.'

Finn pulled Zoe into his arms and enveloped her completely, burying his head in the curls on her neck. He stood, holding onto her, his body racked with sobs.

Chapter 40

7.45pm

After the row with Luke and Martha in the bistro, none of Ellie's group wanted to stay, so she told Alan they'd go home and phone through an order. One of them could nip over and collect it.

By 7.30pm, the whole group was back at the windmill with what remained of their prosecco. Sylvia picked five pizzas off the bistro's online menu and Zoe phoned through the order. Most of them had lost their appetite, so they could share what came.

Finn had gone for a shower and Ellie couldn't relax, so she sneaked upstairs and shut herself in her bedroom. She'd had a text from Dave: someone had reported seeing Brian Silk in Andrea's garden. The police had arrested him and he was now safely in custody.

Phew.

But things had gone badly wrong with Finn and his father, and she felt responsible. If she had told Finn who his dad was, it would still have been awkward, bumping into him in the restaurant, but nowhere near as bad as the shock for Finn of coming face-to-face with the man who either hadn't wanted anything to do with him all his life or who had been told lies to put him off. And, to make matters worse, he'd been with Martha, someone Finn clearly did not like.

Martha had muttered about knowing Luke 'through Andrea'. That didn't work if she and Andrea had only met after they'd had their babies. By then, Luke had parachuted out of Andrea's life.

Poor Finn had even more questions to get answers to now. None of them knew for sure how he had guessed that Luke was his father, but Ellie suspected that he must've heard his mother talk about him when he was little, not realising that he'd taken the name in.

Then there was Bob's information.

If Sue had poisoned Andrea, who had killed *her*?

Ellie wasn't even sure if she believed that Sue had killed Andrea. Sure, Sue had been mean to her, but she had apologised and seemed to have genuinely cared about Andrea in the weeks before her death. It didn't make sense. She needed input from the others.

She padded back downstairs with her laptop. The kitchen smelled of warm cheese.

'Mum? What's the matter?' Zoe came over.

Finn was out of the shower and was sitting at the kitchen table, his head in his hands.

'I cannot for the life of me think of a way of finding out who killed Andrea. Nothing seems to fit.'

Sylvia was engrossed in something on her own laptop's screen but must have heard what Ellie said. 'I know it's not very cheery, but there are quite a few documentaries and dramas and films about people who've poisoned others. We could watch one of those? See if it gives us any ideas?' She looked up. 'There's an episode of *House*, one of *NCIS*, the film *Edge of Darkness*, the film *The Young Poisoner's Handbook*, which is based on the life of the Teacup Poisoner, Graham Frederick Y–'

Something sparked in Ellie's brain. 'What was his name?'

'Graham Frederick Young. Why?'

'On the notepad in Martha's hall, she'd written "Graham's video". It didn't register. I just thought she must have a friend called Graham and she'd borrowed his video or something. Did the Teacup Poisoner definitely use thallium?'

'Yes. According to this. He poisoned loads of people with it in the sixties and seventies.'

'That's got to be too much of a coincidence, surely?' Sally jumped in. 'Someone in the village is poisoned with thallium, and Martha wrote down the first name of one of the most infamous poisoners in history? That must put her in the frame.'

'Perhaps that's where she got the idea from to use thallium?' Sylvia's suggestion was a possibility. 'Maybe she wanted to check out how to use it, and the note was a reminder to get the video?'

It was perfectly possible.

'Has anyone else apart from me raised questions about Martha?' Finn asked. 'What about Debbie? Sue?'

'*Sue.*' It was almost a shout from Ellie. 'Oh my God. *Andrea's journal.* Sue brought it over. I completely forgot.' Ellie scrambled to her feet and dashed into the kitchen to get her bag. She pulled out the cardboard-backed book and turned to the first page. She was silent for a few moments as she skimmed over the pages. Then said, 'I cannot believe what I'm reading! There's page after page here about Martha's bullying. Her threats. Her constant requests to spend time with Finn–'

Finn raised his head. His eyes were bloodshot and his t-shirt was on inside out. 'I can confirm those requests. I don't know how many times I told her I didn't want to.'

Ellie whirled round. 'What did you just say?'

'That I told Martha I didn't want to spend time with her.'

'That's it. It was *Martha* who was giving Andrea a hard time on the phone in the car park at the village hall. In the hairdresser, Jane said she'd overheard Andrea say, "I've told you. He doesn't want to". She was talking to Martha about Finn.'

'Yes. *I* said it. *Mum* said it. Over and over.'

Ellie returned to the journal. 'More pages about Martha's use of coercive control. Guilt-tripping her, belittling her. Pages about Martha's toxic behaviour towards Andrea. Hang on. What's this?'

Halfway through, there was an entry in capital letters and red ink in Sue's handwriting, with a bubble over the 'I'.

Ellie read it out. *'I THINK MARTHA KILLED ANDREA.'*

'Doesn't surprise me one bit.' Finn had got up and had his hands on his hips.

'I'm pretty sure Martha killed Sue too,' Ellie said. 'We need to find something that links her to the castle this morning. If we all search, we might be able to. Finn, Zoe, anyone with a phone. Can you get onto the internet and look for images of Sue and Martha at Wootton Castle between 7am and 10am this morning? At the entrance, on the steps to the moat, or *in* the actual moat.'

Ellie plonked herself down on the sofa and opened her laptop. Zoe, Finn, Sylvia and Sally were soon beside her. Pete had collected their pizzas and was dishing them up.

'There's no point us all checking the same platforms,' Zoe said. 'It's duplicating labour. Finn, you do Facebook. Sally, you do Twitter. Mum, do you want to do Instagram since you use it, and I'll do TikTok? Gran, can you do Google?'

Pete brought their takeaway through and they all settled down to eat and search for images.

Ellie could barely force food down, managing a few mouthfuls before giving up. She scrolled through as many hashtags and public accounts on Instagram as she could think of. Wootton Castle, Kent castles, Deal, interest groups, castles, tourism, anything that felt remotely relevant. It felt like they were looking for two particular pebbles on a massive beach. She scrolled and clicked, on and on, her fingers and wrists aching.

Then she clicked on a public post from a history group in Canterbury. They had gone on a visit to Wootton Castle this morning. Yep, the date was right. And time-stamped at 8.45am. It was a composite post showing several images. The minibus arriving. The group members getting out. Crossing the road. The group lined up, excited faces, waiting to go into the castle.

And there it was, plain as day.

Sue and Martha behind the group, going through the metal gates and down the stone steps into the moat. In the gaps, Ellie could just make out Lily the spaniel.

'I've got it,' she screamed. 'Unless it's a complete coincidence – evidence of who killed Sue. Two people went down into that moat and only one came up alive. Martha.'

They were all staring at her.

'You're kidding?' Zoe said.

'Nope.'

Zoe leaped up and squished herself in next to her mum.

Ellie turned the laptop around so they could see. 'History group trip, with Martha and Sue in the background. Boom.' She paused to gather her thoughts. 'Finn, I need to talk to you in private.'

Finn gaped at her. 'O-kaay.'

'Pete, can you run over to the bistro and see if Martha and Luke are still there?'

'Sure.'

'Zoe, can you phone your dad and tell him to meet us at the bistro in an hour, or at Martha's house if we aren't there. If Luke isn't there, ask your dad to get him over to Martha's too.'

'Cool.'

'I'll call Alan and let him know we're on our way over. We'll need Bob, as he's the executor of Andrea's will, and Debbie.' Ellie sat back for a moment. She couldn't believe the nightmare was almost over.

First, though, she needed to talk to Finn about his mother. Then she needed to get the slip of paper from the jeep that she tore off Martha's notepad.

Chapter 41

9pm

Ellie knew they needed to get to the bistro quickly so that she could confront Martha with the things they had discovered. But when she, Finn, Zoe, Sally and Sylvia arrived, it was too late. Martha and Luke had already left. They would have to all go to Martha's. She texted Dave – just in case he hadn't got Zoe's message – and asked him to come to the Priest House in three quarters of an hour.

Fifteen minutes later, they had blagged their way into Martha's living room. Sally and Sylvia sat on a sofa. Zoe and Finn were on a window seat. The light from the snow through the patio doors was almost too beautiful. On the huge wooden mantelpiece, the white fairy lights twinkled. Below, orange flames flickered in the inglenook fireplace, with an occasional crackle and spit from the logs.

'What's going on?' Martha looked first at Ellie, then at the faces of everyone present. 'I thought you said Finn wanted to apologise for ruining our meal?'

'You'll find out in a second,' Ellie replied.

Alan, Bob and Debbie filed in and took up positions by the wall.

'I know you've morphed into Miss Marple lately, Ellie, but could someone please tell me what you all are doing here?' Martha sneered. She was by the fire and Luke was in a leather chair nearby.

Ellie had planned her questions and anticipated the objections. 'We are all here because two people have been killed. Many of us in this room had disputes and fallouts with Andrea, but only one person wanted her dead. Some might have gained from killing her. But only *one* of us went from *thinking* about it to *actually doing* it.'

Ellie focused on Debbie. 'It's true, isn't it, that you were very angry when your sister changed her will to include Finn?'

'Well, initially,' Debbie stammered, 'yes.'

'And that you wanted to challenge the will so as to be able to pay off your husband's debts?'

Everyone's attention was on Debbie.

'You've made no secret of your low opinion of Finn,' Ellie continued. 'You've kept hinting about him only being after Andrea's money. That he wasn't going to hang around. How violent he'd been around her.'

Debbie spluttered.

'But I don't think you went as far as wanting your sister out of the way.'

'I most certainly did not.' Debbie glanced over at Finn. He and Zoe were side by side. 'It's true that I've said and thought those things. But not quite in the way that you're suggesting. I loved my sister. And I watched her struggle for years. First, when the man she loved married someone else...,' she glanced in Ellie's direction, '...and then when the father of her child didn't *seem* to want anything to do with her – or him.'

Luke sighed. He uncrossed his legs and crossed them again the other way.

Debbie looked pleadingly at Finn, who was leaning against a wall, absorbing every word that poured from his aunt's mouth. 'But it's also true that my views have changed.'

She stopped and addressed Finn directly. 'What I've realised these past few days is how much pain *you* were in yourself. I was so focused, first on my sister, then on my husband, that I don't think I noticed that. And I'm really sorry.' She stopped briefly. 'When she was alive, I wanted her to have enough income for herself. I was upset to see you spending what was effectively her money on drugs and alcohol.'

'I don't take drugs any more.' Finn's voice was soft. 'And I actually had several part-time jobs when I was living with Mum. So, the money I spent on drugs was my own. But...,' he paused, 'I'll admit there's some truth in what you say. I probably wasn't as caring towards Mum as I could have been. I regret that now. I didn't give much consideration to how things were for her. I know I've been selfish.' He placed his hand on his heart.

Ellie shifted her gaze from Finn to Debbie. 'You guys will have time to build bridges.' She was looking at Finn's father now. 'Luke, you've had a lot of experience playing detective.'

'Indeed.'

'But you're very much a reluctant participant here. In fact, if Sylvia hadn't tracked your film set down, and we hadn't bumped into you in the bistro, we might still be wondering where you are in all of this.'

His eyes narrowed and he gave a lazy shrug.

'You give the impression of being the consummate professional. The slick actor. But you don't seem to cope with the relationships in your life which are inconvenient. The ones that are *messier* than you'd like.' She carried on quickly before he seized the chance to intervene. 'Isn't it true that you saw red when Andrea announced to you not just that she was dying, but that she wanted you to include your son in your life and your wealth?'

Luke cleared his throat. He stood up and sauntered over to the fireplace, hands in the pockets of his corduroy trousers. 'It's true, I didn't take her demands well. I didn't want to be a father when she got pregnant, and although it was her right to go through with the pregnancy, I wasn't prepared to be bounced into playing a role I wasn't comfortable with.' He didn't look at Finn. He began pacing across the carpet as he spoke, ever the actor on stage. 'I know that makes me very selfish. I *have* been an absent father, and I wasn't prepared to step up when Andrea got in touch a few weeks ago, any more than I did when she first got pregnant. At least not in the way she wanted.' He held his hands up over his head as though surrendering. 'Every time I asked Martha about Finn, she told me most emphatically that he had no desire to see me. I suppose that made things a bit simpler. So, if it helps, *mea culpa*. I'm happy to be the bad guy here. But I have never wanted Andrea dead.'

'I'm glad you've mentioned Martha.' Finn's words sliced through the air. He was standing up squarely now. 'How did your friendship come about exactly? You've somehow kept in touch with her and not with my mother.'

'You mean, *she's* kept in touch with *me*. Bounced me into coming along to the Bakery Book Club too. Well, as you've probably realised by now, when Martha wants something, she gets it.' He rubbed the back of his neck. 'When you were born, Andrea told Martha who I was. Martha managed to contact me and said that if I ever had anything to do with you, she would tell my fiancée – who's now my wife – about you. I couldn't risk that happening.'

Martha shot Luke a look of daggers and flicked invisible specks of dust off her sleeve. 'I must say, Ellie, this little charade is *priceless*. I can't decide whether you've finally lost your marbles or whether you're actually being serious. Do you really expect me to believe that this is what we are all doing here? If you're going to accuse all of us of murdering Andrea, we are going to be here some time. I think I'll get myself a nice glass of fizz and–'

'Not *everyone*, no.' Ellie's voice was firm. 'You see, upstairs in your wardrobe you have photos which tell a very different story from the one you've been telling everybody in the village.' Ellie got out her phone.

Panic flashed across Martha's face. 'What photos?'

'I have copies here. Sally, would you go and fetch the originals, please?'

Sally slipped out of the room.

'What are you talking about?' Martha tried to smile and laugh, to soften her voice. 'You can't do that.' She stared at Ellie.

'*This* photo. Of you and Andrea with your babies, Nate and Finn.' She passed her phone to Martha. 'You see, I realised something was off on the downs the other day when you denied knowing Andrea before you moved to Lower Wootton. It was a careless lie, wasn't it?'

'I don't know what you're talking about.'

'The photo shows that the two of you have been friends–'

'*If* you can call it that,' hissed Debbie from across the room.

'...since you both had your babies. Isn't that true?'

Sally arrived back, clutching the photographs that Ellie and Sally had seen in Martha's wardrobe.

'Thank you. Could you give them to Bob, please?'

She passed the images across.

Ellie gave a reassuring smile to Sue's husband. 'Alan, could you tell everyone what you told me about Sue?'

'Happy to.' He threw a rage-filled glance in Martha's direction. 'In the last few months, I've watched my wife go from being a kind, sensitive woman into a nervous wreck, all thanks to you. Initially, it was because of something she overheard *you* saying to Andrea one day when she was doing one of Ellie's cleaning jobs.'

'Oh joy,' sneered Martha. 'More deluded ramblings. I'm looking forward to hearing this.'

'You see, my wife heard you bully Andrea over this young man. You didn't know she was there. She was on the floor, on her hands and knees, cleaning the skirting boards, and you started on at Andrea, demanding that she let you spend time with Finn.'

'Your wife must have been mistaken.'

'She definitely was not. Had it been one isolated comment, perhaps, but it wasn't. She heard the *whole conversation*. You telling Andrea that she owed you, because your son died and Finn was still alive.'

Everyone gasped, and all eyes were on Martha.

'Andrea felt desperate. She couldn't cope with you constantly trying to make her feel guilty. Telling her what to do and trying to control her. She wasn't a pet or a plaything. I know she felt like this because she confided in Sue. Told her all about your toxic behaviour and about the cancer. After that, Andrea became more and more reliant on her.'

'It's not true. He's mad.'

'I'm afraid it is true,' Alan continued. 'Sue knew Andrea was keeping a journal–'

'And – if the police have any doubt about what Alan's saying, *voilà*.' Ellie produced the diary from her bag and turned to face Martha. 'This is Andrea's journal. Stream-of-consciousness stuff at first. Then, a systematic recording of all the agonising developments in your campaign to cosy up to Finn and to prise him away from her. It charts your descent from an unhealthy preoccupation to an all-consuming obsession. And yet, all the time, you've pretended to be Andrea's friend.'

Martha's face was like thunder. 'Where did you get that from?' She lunged at Ellie. 'Give that to me.'

Ellie snatched the journal out of her reach. 'I don't think so. It's not yours to have. But I will tell you where I got it from. Before Sue died–' She stopped. 'Let's try that again. Before Sue was *killed*, she dropped it up to the windmill.'

Luke's voice reverberated around the room. 'Where did Sue get it from?'

'That's an excellent question. When I arrived at the Priest House the evening Andrea died, someone was leaving. It took me a while to find out who. First, I assumed it was Finn. But he hasn't got a motorbike. Then I discovered Debbie had a BMW bike. However, when Sue told me she was scared, and asked me to go to the police station with her, I couldn't figure out why. In fact, she was so scared, and so determined to safeguard the information in this journal, that she collected it on her scooter the night Andrea was killed and dropped it off to me this morning. So it was Sue's scooter I heard that night.'

Ellie addressed Martha now. 'This journal lays out all the details of your vile behaviour, going right back to what happened at the hospital when your babies were born.'

'*That* is none of your business.' Martha's nostrils were flaring.

'But it is. Because it's where your antipathy towards Andrea began and has been the basis for the obsession you developed with Finn – and her.'

Ellie looked at Finn and gave a warm smile. 'It's OK, Martha. I've told him. I wouldn't want him stumbling on your secret without warning.'

Bob held up the photograph of Martha and Andrea with Finn and Nate.

'Do you want to tell everyone what happened before this photo was taken?' Ellie asked Martha. 'At the hospital?'

'I have no idea what you're talking about.'

Ellie faced the room. 'It was Nate's hair that gave it away, and the journal confirms it.'

Martha's lips were pressed tightly together.

'You see, Andrea's son, Finn, and your son, Nate, were born in the same hospital. On the same ward, in fact, and you and she became friends. But before you both left hospital, there was a mix-up, and you took the wrong babies home.'

There was a collective intake of breath in the room.

Ellie spoke to Martha directly now. 'I'm sure hospital records will confirm it all for the police, but it's in the journal too. You took *Finn* home, didn't you?'

Finn covered his face with his hands. 'I can't bear it.' The words came out with force.

'And Andrea took Nate home. That mix-up was the beginning of your madness, wasn't it? The hospital didn't discover the error for several weeks. When they notified you and Andrea, you both agreed to swap the babies back. But whereas Andrea *had* bonded with Nate, you hadn't bonded with Finn, had you? Was this what sparked your jealousy?'

'It wasn't like that.' Martha's eyes darted with fury. 'But I don't expect you to understand.'

'And when Andrea bonded with baby Finn, you couldn't bear it. Could you? And you couldn't bond with Nate either because you were so obsessed with Finn.'

'Nate deserved so much better than a mother like you,' Finn snarled at Martha.

'Isn't it true that you've been obsessed with Finn since he was a baby? And that it got worse when Nate died?'

'You wouldn't understand.' Martha stomped over to the window.

'Isn't it true that you moved to Lower Wootton to be closer to Finn? Where all you could think about was trying to persuade him to spend time with you. At first, I didn't see it. Nate and Finn both started life blond. Finn stayed fair. Like Luke. But Nate's hair grew gradually darker.'

'So what?' Martha snarled.

'In the newborn photos, you held Finn, and Andrea held Nate. When you'd swapped your babies back, it was the same, of course. But in the photographs of Nate when he was about five, his hair had gone mousey, then light brown by the time he was ten. And it made me realise that if your babies had somehow got swapped, you might not have known.' Ellie faced Martha again. 'I kept wondering, what if you'd taken the wrong babies home? Started to raise the wrong children? I thought perhaps it might explain some of the difficulties.'

'Those tests were never right. The hospital made a mistake. Finn was *my* son. Andrea kept him from me.' Martha spat the words. 'None of you understand what it's like to be rejected by the baby you love.' She looked over at Finn. 'When I put my arms round you, you cried.'

'Because I never felt safe with you.' His honesty was brutal.

'That's ridiculous.' Martha spun round to address Ellie. 'The information in that journal is private,' said Martha. 'You had no right to read it.'

'I think you'll find *that* is down to Andrea's executor to decide,' Ellie replied. 'And we have him in the room. Bob?'

Bob shuffled forward. 'I shall be handing the photos and journal over to the police.'

'What I cannot get over is that when Nate died, you thought Andrea *owed* you. You vowed to make her pay and to get what you believed was yours: Finn. Did you get rid of Andrea so that you could finally have Finn to yourself?' Ellie asked. 'You'd seen him back in the village and you couldn't bear it. You couldn't wait a moment longer...'

'I just wanted what was rightfully mine.' Her voice was barely audible. 'Andrea said she had a couple of years to live but you know what it's like. People say that and they go on living for ten years. I'd waited long enough. I wanted my son.'

'You're sick. You need help.' Anger had spread across Finn's face.

'And you told Luke that Finn had no interest in seeing him. Presumably, that was to extinguish the already remote chance of poor Finn getting to meet his father.'

'Oh God,' Luke muttered. 'The film set.' He must finally have realised who Sally and Sylvia were.

Ellie continued. 'And you killed Andrea to get Finn.'

'Absolutely not.'

'Are you familiar with the Teacup Poisoner and the film, *The Young Poisoner's Handbook*?'

'I have no idea what you're talking about.'

'The "Teacup Poisoner" was the nickname that was given to Graham Frederick Young, who poisoned lots of people with thallium in the sixties and seventies. In your hall, you have a notepad. On it was the imprint of writing from the slip above which had been removed.'

From her jeans, Ellie produced the piece of paper. 'It says "GRAHAM'S VIDEO". When the police search your house, I'd put money on them finding a copy of that video.'

Martha made a move for the door, but Bob got there first and blocked her path.

Ellie passed the slip of paper to him. 'In the journal, Sue wrote, "I think Martha killed Andrea". Sue went on to write that she visited Andrea two days before she died. She was in bed with migraine. Sue left her keys on the bedside table next to a mug of tea.'

Ellie smiled at Bob. 'This is what you told us. What you didn't know – which Sue explains in the journal – is that *Martha* had made the tea and brought it in to Andrea.'

She spun round to face Martha. '*You* slipped thallium into the drink, didn't you?'

Martha was silent.

At that moment, Dave appeared at the patio doors. His hair and coat were covered with snow. Ellie let him in and he stood at the side of the room.

'What about Sue's death?' Alan asked.

'We found a public photograph on Instagram of Sue, Martha and Lily the spaniel going down into the moat at the castle at 8.45am this morning.' Ellie swiped her phone and brought up the image. 'Time and date stamped.' She passed the phone to Alan.

'I thought she was killed because of what she knew,' he said. 'Now I know I was right.'

'Sue made another entry for us to find in Andrea's journal. That she'd asked Martha to meet her in a public place – at the castle – so she could confront her with what she knew and tell her that time was up. Martha had to go to the police. Sue felt guilty for the mean things she'd said to Andrea, and that she *felt* she'd let her down. She wanted to help put things right by getting justice.'

'But Martha had other ideas,' Alan added.

'As for the forensics, and what exactly happened in the moat, I'll leave that to the police,' Ellie said, looking in Dave's direction. 'Staff and other witnesses may already have confirmed that the two of them were at the castle together.'

'Did you push her down the stone steps?' Alan shouted at Martha. 'Have a row and bash her over the head?'

Martha walked towards Ellie and stopped, her face inches from Ellie's.

Dave shot forward.

'You really are the village curtain twitcher, aren't you?' Martha snorted.

'Not really. Just someone who objects to good people being murdered in cold blood.'

'A real little snoop,' Martha continued. 'No wonder this useless waste of space ran off and left you.' She gestured to Dave. 'What's the expression? Make sure you keep the home fires burning? Still, I always thought he had a roving eye.'

Dave stepped forward. 'Martha McVey, I am arresting you on suspicion of murdering Sue Patterson. You do not have to say anything...'

Chapter 42

Day 4 – 24th Dec, 7pm

Ellie, Zoe and Sylvia were in the village hall waiting for *Cinderella* to start. Ellie was so excited, she barely noticed how hard the plastic seats were. The room was buzzing. Every place was full and there were even people standing at the back.

'Ladies and gentlemen, may we wish you a warm welcome to tonight's very special Christmas Eve performance of *Cinderella*.' Mike, the am dram director, was on the stage. With his black tuxedo and new haircut, he was unrecognisable from the last time Ellie saw him. He beamed out at the audience from in front of the curtain. 'Jane and I would like to say thank you on behalf of the Wootton Players for coming along this evening, and for your patience while we reallocated tickets.' He pointed to the back of the room. 'Thanks must also go to Finn

Burdett for introducing standing room tickets for the first time ever.' Mike gestured to the sound booth where Finn was rolling up cables.

Zoe nudged her mum in the seat next to her and grinned proudly.

Ellie took in the hall. The set was stunning.

Sally whispered. 'What an amazing job they've made.'

'Shh,' hissed Sylvia.

Jane joined Mike on the stage and took over. 'We are, of course, without two very important people this evening, and they will be very much missed from our future productions. That's Andrea Burdett and Sue Patterson. And this production is dedicated to both of them.'

'Now, we'll hand over to our wonderful actors,' Mike said proudly. 'Ladies and gentlemen, may I present this year's panto, *Cinderella.*'

Chapter 43

Day 5– 25th Dec, 1pm

Ellie added the final extra chair to the dining table. She lit the beautiful white candles, brought by Sally and Pete, then stood back to admire the effect. Dappled sunlight streamed in through the tiny windows from both sides of the windmill, pooling on the white tablecloth.

The places were set. Zoe, Finn, Sally, Pete, Sylvia and Sue's husband, Alan. One of Pete's posh, gold crackers lay above each person's dessert cutlery. Two water jugs and a cluster of tumblers. Wine glasses. Serving spoons. The turkey was out of the oven, and they were all looking forward to their traditional Christmas dinner.

It had been a year since Dave had admitted his affair and agreed to leave. It had been a year since Ellie had had this many people around the dining table. She and Zoe perched at one end of it sometimes, but this was different. And, for the first time in ages, she liked the way it felt. Liked the whole of their gorgeous home being used again. It was, of course, true that the day was tinged with great sadness. Finn had lost his mother and Alan had lost his wife.

Ellie fiddled with the floral display that Sally and Pete had made with flowers from the garden centre. Mouse, Andrea's cat, jumped up onto a chair and meowed. Ellie gave her a stroke.

'Shall we have a bottle of wine at each end?' Zoe's question broke Ellie's musings.

'That's a good idea.'

Zoe had a bag of party poppers under her arm, and she sprinkled them around the table. When she finished, Ellie enveloped her daughter in a huge hug. 'I'm so pleased you're feeling better, darling. It's the best Christmas present.'

'Thanks, Mum.'

'I'm sorry it's been such a tough year.' Ellie gave a weary smile. 'Next year's going to be better for the Blixes. I *know* it.' She made a triumphant arm gesture and they both laughed.

'I feel it too.' Zoe was chewing her cheek pensively. 'I'm glad everything is out in the open.'

From the kitchen, Finn called.

Ellie was miles away but Zoe caught his question. 'Finn says can do presents now.'

'Yup. Give me a couple of minutes. How is he?'

'He was really upset earlier. He was having a little cry in the bathroom.'

There was a rap at the front door.

'Get that, love, will you?' Ellie said to Zoe. 'I'll be there in a sec.'

Zoe scuttled back to the kitchen to answer the door.

Ellie focused her attention on the table again. She'd been pleased when Alan said he'd join them, and that he wasn't going to be on his own. Like Finn, it would take him time to come to terms with what had happened. Rebus, however, was thrilled to have Lily to play with.

In the kitchen, the dogs were barking excitedly and Ellie could hear the clack of claws on the wooden floor. Must have been someone they knew at the door.

'Mumm?' Zoe called. 'You're wanted.'

Ellie stared up at the spiral staircase, admiring the nightlights-in-jars that Zoe had placed on each tread of the stairs, and the trail of fairy lights that Finn had run along the base of the sofas. Then she turned towards the kitchen and found herself looking straight at Dave.

A cherry-red scarf lay on the collar of his pea coat. Melting snow speckled his hair. Zoe was draped over her dad's arm, beaming at her mum.

Ellie's stomach somersaulted. 'Oh. Hi.'

Over by the kitchen cabinets, Finn, Sally, Pete, Sylvia and Alan stood in a row, all watching, as still as sentry men.

Ellie didn't have a clue what to do or what to say. 'Have you ... have you,' she stammered, '...come for Zoe?'

'No, no.' His arms were across his chest, nervous, presumably, like her. He gave a nod to the group who were watching him. 'Mum.'

'Come in, come in,' Sylvia said warmly.

Finn followed. 'Yes, we're just about to have some fizz, Mr Blix. Would you like to join us?'

'That's very kind.' He smiled at them both. 'But no. Simon and Jen are at mine, so I'll not stop.'

What was he doing here then?

'I ... er... just wanted to...' He hesitated and focused his eyes on Ellie, '...to wish you a Merry Christmas. And to introduce you to our newest family member.' He opened his coat. There, nestling inside, was a mass of curly fur. A tiny head bobbed up and a puppy wriggled, squealing loudly. It was a blonde cockerpoo.

'Simon and Jen wanted to stick to your naming tradition. She's inquisitive and determined so they've called her Agatha.' He extracted the puppy from his coat and placed her in Ellie's arms. 'Here. Take her.'

'Aww.' Ellie folded her hands around the warm, wriggling body. The bundle of innocent excitement. She sunk her nose into Agatha's soft fur. 'Oh, my goodness.' She drew the puppy up to her face, and when she felt the fur against her skin, she couldn't stop the tears from coming. 'Thank you.' She kissed the puppy's nose and whispered into her coat.

'She's jabbed. It's OK for her to...' Dave pointed at Rebus and Lily on the ground. 'It was just the snow on her tiny paws.'

Ellie crouched down and showed the older dogs the puppy. 'Who's this, Reeby? Lily? Meet your niece, little Agatha.'

Rebus stuffed his face into the puppy's tummy and received a jab on the nose from a pudgy paw.

Ellie opened her arms so Agatha could decide what she wanted to do. Quick as a flash, she was down on the floor, on her back, rolling around Rebus' paws, nipping at his feet and chewing Lily's long spaniel ears.

Zoe was quickly kneeling beside the dogs, supervising.

Ellie got to her feet and walked towards Dave. She grabbed her duffle coat from the rack and gently ushered him towards the front door. She wanted to ... to what? She didn't really know.

Outside, the two of them stood in the windmill doorway.

'Thanks for bringing the puppy over to show me. It was really kind.'

'There's another reason I came over. We got interrupted the other day.'

Ellie's heart lurched. 'Is this about Andrea?'

'Yes.' He was looking straight at her. Ellie saw her own pain reflected in his eyes. 'She told me she'd contacted you. We saw the email on her computer and know she died before you guys got to talk.'

An image flashed through Ellie's mind, of Andrea shouting through the letterbox at her the week before. 'Yes, well, part of that's my fault.'

'It's OK. She understood. She obviously wasn't expecting to die the way she has. But she said if she did die before she'd spoken to you, she asked me to tell you what she'd wanted to say.'

'Her email said something about it not being just about her and me.'

Dave gently rested his hands on Ellie's shoulders, and Ellie got the impression that he was determined this time to say the things he needed to. 'When I finished things with her, I told her why. I told her I still loved you.' His eyes were on Ellie's. 'I *do* still love you.' He paused, allowing her to take in his words. 'And I told her I'd made a mistake.'

Ellie heard a loud gasp behind the door, then giggling and Zoe whispering.

'Clear off, you lot,' she yelled over her shoulder. 'Haven't you heard of privacy?'

Dave wasn't deterred. 'That's what she wanted to tell you. She felt really bad that you and I broke up, when I didn't love her.' He paused. 'When you said you wanted a divorce, and told me not to contact you–'

'You had an affair. I was hurt.' Ellie dropped her head. This was too much.

'I know. And I am really, *really* sorry.' His voice was gentle and it made Ellie's heart melt. 'What I'm saying is, Andrea wanted you to know the truth, in case it helped.'

Ellie was processing the news. She didn't know how she felt about it. 'OK. Well, thanks for telling me.' She exhaled. 'Finally.' But in the recesses of her mind, a question was still determined to surface. 'The call you got. Who's Ruby?'

'She's one of the CSIs at work.'

'Are you seeing her?' Ellie felt like she was going to throw up.

He didn't answer straightaway. 'No.' He paused. 'But – she's hinted that that's what she wants.'

'Plenty of women will jump at the chance of having a fella like him'. Sally's words rang in Ellie's ears.

She was losing him. 'What do *you* want?'

From inside the windmill, Ellie heard the puppy's high-pitched barks. The hubbub of chatter.

'I don't know.' He removed his hands from Ellie's shoulders and closed his eyes, confusion written on his face. 'The truth is that until a couple of years ago, I'd never envisaged being with anyone except you. Never imagined a *life* without you. I don't believe in all that "other half" stuff, but we've always been "Ellie and Dave". I honestly thought we'd grow old together; be grandparents. My life doesn't feel complete without you.'

'But?'

'Look, there's no blame here. I have a busy life. So do you. But we seemed to have become mates who just jog along. And I was feeling – increasingly – like you didn't love me any more. I mean, like a husband, like a man. And it's not about sex, in case you're thinking that. I just didn't–' His voice broke, and his eyes filled up. He heaved in a sigh. The tears rolled down his cheeks. Suddenly, his voice burst from his chest. 'I didn't think you loved me any more.'

His words hit Ellie and suddenly it all made sense. 'And Andrea did,' she said softly.

'I know it makes me sound like a pathetic, needy bloke who has an affair and blames his wife...'

That's not how it was. It was what he'd said the other day.

'I'm not blaming you. I'm really not. It's just *how I felt.*' His voice was still thick with emotion. 'I did have an affair. But I quickly realised it was the stupidest thing I've ever done.'

Ellie was taking in what he was saying. The words were like balm and she wanted to listen to them forever. But he had hurt her deeply, and she was going to need time to process, to heal, to think about what she wanted. 'I'm glad you came over. Thank you. It's a huge relief to know how you feel.'

His eyes were searching her face and part of her wanted to melt into him.

'Zoe's going over to yours later. I expect Finn will go with her.'

'You know where I am now.'

'Goose Meadow.' Ellie liked the way it sounded.

'I don't want to go back, Ellie.'

'I don't want to, either.'

'Perhaps we can–'

'Mu-um,' came Zoe's voice from inside the windmill. 'The puppy's peed on the rug.'

Ellie laughed. 'Let's talk again. I think that's our cue.'

Dave placed his hand on Ellie's cheek.

Ellie savoured his touch for a few moments before speaking. 'Coming,' she replied to Zoe.

*

Half an hour later, Dave and the puppy had left, and everyone was around the table, chatting and laughing. Zoe, Finn, Sally, Pete, Sylvia and Alan.

The landline rang and Zoe ran to answer it. She brought the receiver over. 'It's Simon.'

'Happy Christmas, Mum!' He sounded tipsy and cheerful.

'Hey, Happy Christmas,' Ellie said. 'You beat me to it. How are you?'

They chatted away, and before he rang off, Simon said he and Jen would pop over tomorrow.

Everyone resumed their conversations. Ellie sat quietly, watching, listening in occasionally. She sipped her prosecco, reflecting on the madness of the last few days. The carols on the green seemed ages ago. She vividly remembered feeling that all she had wanted was to keep her head down and make it through the festive season. But something had shifted, and now she felt glimmers of hope.

She had no idea what would happen with Dave, and that was OK, because she felt hopeful about herself and her own life.

She twirled the stem of her glass between her fingers and looked around the table at the happy, smiling faces. A wave of love washed over her for her family and her wonderful friends in the village.

THE END.

About the author

Izzie Harper is the pen name of writer, teacher & story coach, Vicky Newham. Vicky lives on the south coast of England.

As Izzie Harper, she writes The Wootton Windmill Mysteries. The first of these, *Murder at the Christmas Carols*, was published on 21st November 2022. The second will be out in 2023.

Vicky's first crime fiction series was published by HQ/Harper Collins. Her debut in this series, *Turn a Blind Eye*, was optioned for TV and was shortlisted for the CWA John Creasey Debut Dagger in 2019. She has MAs in Creative Writing and Effective Learning.

Vicky divides her time between writing and teaching. She is passionate about helping other writers to craft their stories, and to make informed decisions about their publishing paths.

To keep up to date with Vicky's releases, special offers and promotions, please join her book club here.

If you like pictures of dogs, the sea, the Kent countryside and behind-the-scenes of Vicky's writing, you can follow her on Twitter at @VickyNewham and on Instagram at @vickynewhamwriter.

If you have enjoyed this story, Vicky would be hugely grateful if you could leave a quick review on Amazon and if you could tell your family and friends about it. Reviews and word-of-mouth recommendations are the *best* way to help authors.

Acknowledgements

When I was growing up, I adored reading Enid Blyton. The books were such fun and I longed to climb through the pages and join the characters on their adventures. I quickly moved onto Agatha Christie. When I was studying for my French A-level, I read Georges Simenon. With Christie and Simenon, it wasn't about the adventure. It was about the puzzle and the detection. All three authors set off a lifelong love affair with mysteries. I have continued to read them prolifically – and adore writing them.

During the COVID pandemic and associated lockdowns, I found myself wanting to write stories which were lighter in tone than my previous gritty, urban police procedurals. I didn't want to write gory corpse scenes, or go into detail about murder methods and forensics. I wanted to write about a community where people cared about each other. I wanted to write stories which featured warmth, humour and friendship more prominently. And I wanted to write about characters who aren't constrained by police procedures. Characters who can get away with the things that detectives cannot.

This is where I got the idea for the Wootton Windmill Mysteries. I moved house during one of the UK lockdowns and across the fields from where I live in Kent is a 'smock' windmill. If you look on my social media, you'll see some photos of it. I kept thinking about what an amazing home it would be for my main character. Ripple Windmill isn't converted into a home. It's been lovingly restored by the owners to a working mill. No longer in use, except for open days. I have moved the mill, and many other local landmarks, to create my fictional village of Lower Wootton.

I hope you enjoy reading about these characters as much as I am enjoying writing about them.

Please note: I am a British writer and write using British English. The manuscript has been edited by British editors. A few spellings, terms and words may therefore be different for some readers.

Writing a novel is a team effort. I come up with the plot and characters, and write the words, but other people contribute at various stages. Without their input and magic, this story would not have made it into print.

I owe massive thanks to the following people for their help. To each of you, please know that I appreciate you. You are, in no particular order: David Penny (without whom I would probably still be talking about finishing this story), Roz Watkins (sorry about the flower bed and I have a watch now), Louise Mangos (unacknowledged chainsaw expert), Lisa Hall (plot-while-we-swim sessions are *the* best), Dionne Lister, Sara Starbuck, Louise Voss, Gemma Pettman and another lovely person (please say thank you), Steven Dunne, Jules Swain, Lynne Francis, Dave Sivers, Victoria Goldman, Lynne Milford, Rebecca Bradley and Neil Lancaster. Apologies to anyone I've temporarily forgotten.

*